A BRIEF CANDLE

About Notion Press

Notion Press is a Self-Publishing platform to write, publish & sell Print books and eBooks around the world. To learn more, visit www.notionpress.com

A BRIEF CANDLE is a product of the Notion Press Author Incubation Program.

A BRIEF CANDLE

PRADEEP GULATI

notionpress.com

NotionPress

5 Muthu Kalathy Street, Triplicane, Chennai - 600005

First Published by NotionPress

ISBN: 978-93-83185-02-3

Disclaimer

All characters in the stories included in this book are fictitious and bear no resemblance to anyone living or dead. All incidents in the stories are purely imaginary and work of fiction. Any resemblance to anything whatsoever and anyone whosoever is purely coincidental.

It is not intended to hurt the feelings of any profession, nationality or community through the contents of this book.

To Anju,

the inspiration for this book, without whom it would not have been written

and

To Kanika

the encouragement without which it would not have been published

Love is a tragic song;
it has a beginning but no end.
Life is a flower, of which love is
the nectar.

December 1982, Ghent, Belgium

The pilot who boarded our ship yesterday morning at Austin brought the mail packet with him and a special letter. A letter that was very special for me. I read the letter again as I had been doing all night; in fact, I had not slept a wink the whole night. I could not; I was too excited. The moment I had been waiting for these many years had finally arrived.

Anju had left India, and me, in 1980. Well, not exactly left me, because there was no way she could ever escape my thoughts. It was just that she had migrated to London, while I was still studying in Calcutta. We had been corresponding regularly while I was in college, almost as frequently as a letter a week, but now that I was working at sea, I made up for the reduced frequency by writing longer letters.

Normally, she began her letters with "Dear Vicky," or, "Dearest Vicky," but this one began with "My Dear Vicky." I suppose absence does make the heart grow fonder ... It would not be long before we took the holy vows and pledged to cherish each other till death parted us. In another three months, I would be signing off the ship and going home. Shortly after that, she would be mine.

Outside, the sun was just rising, spreading its warm glow over the earth and bathing everything in its golden light. She wrote that I should contact her when I reached Ghent and she would board the first available flight from London to Antwerp. As soon as I had received the letter I had obtained permission from the Captain for her to board the ship. The Captain had even offered to arrange for me to go to Antwerp with the ship's agent to meet her at the airport.

I had called her the evening before. Her flight would be arriving at Antwerp at eleven this morning. I looked at my watch for the thousandth time: the hands hardly moved! Time has a habit of moving at a snail's pace when you are waiting for something terrific to happen. The ship's agent promised to drive me to Antwerp about nine o'clock. That was three hours away! My heart was brimming with joy and anticipation at the thought of seeing my sweetheart again – her tender eyes, her lovely face. How I wished the hours would turn to minutes, the minutes to seconds, the seconds to *that* awaited moment. Then, time could stop forever!

I cannot describe how I felt when I received her letter, but I evidently made quite a racket, for the other people living on my deck posted "No Admission" signs on their doors!

I remember vividly how she cried the day before her departure. I cried, too, and she kissed me – our second kiss. I cried again during the night, when I was alone in my room.

At the airport, before passing through security, she held my hand and said, "You won't forget me, Vicky, will you?"

I replied, "You know I won't, Anju. When I become a marine engineer and my ship sails into England, and ... and ..."

"I'll wait for you, Vicky. I will."

As tears blurred my vision, she and her parents were gone.

For a year after that I was busy with studies. About fifteen months ago I started working professionally, and now the moment I promised had arrived. Well. Almost; Belgium was just an hour away from England.

I should get dressed properly, I thought, and felt a tingling sensation. Every part of my body seemed synchronized with my heart. By eight o'clock I stood in front of the mirror dabbing Jovan's Musk Oil After Shave on my face.

Breakfast was a hurried affair. I could not eat! The agent had arrived on board and was in conference with the Captain. Everyone seemed to care about my happiness. First, there were my fellow shipmates who kept staring at me with smug smiles on their faces. Then, the Chief Engineer had considerately given me a day off from duty. Now, the

Captain was arranging my passage to Antwerp with the agent. Life was good!

Finally, the agent came out of the conference room and winked at me.

"Well, sir, let's go," he said.

It was cold on the way to Antwerp, and it began snowing lightly. The warm sun disappeared, and a dull grey sky replaced it.

I wondered if Anju had changed. Had she started wearing lipstick? Was she still the same? She would have boarded her flight at Heathrow by now.

I'll take her out to lunch in style, I decided. *After all, I'm a Merchant Navy officer now.*

The trees by the motorway looked naked without their leaves. Snow was having little success in clothing them in white, but the little cottages we passed seemed to be happy homes, with smoke rising from their chimneys. If I could, I decided, I would eventually settle down somewhere in Europe. Anju often wrote that she liked Europe, especially the countryside.

The radio was playing a song about someone coming home. The agent looked at me and grinned.

"Well, Mr. Sood," he said, "just one more hour."

I smiled back.

"If you please, it would give me real pleasure to make arrangements for both of you to accompany a sightseeing tour tomorrow.

Ghent is a beautiful place with its castles and museums, canals and markets. Our Castle of the Counts dates back to the fifteenth century and our St. Bavo's Cathedral is one of the finest in the world," he informed me. "You can see the famous masterpiece by the Van Eyck brothers, 'The Adoration of the Lamb', and you can take a boat ride in the city's canal ..."

By the time we entered Antwerp's airport, it was almost 10:45 a.m. Fifteen minutes to go ...

It was a small airport, looking more like a cottage from the outside. There was hardly anyone around, just more visitors like myself awaiting their loved ones, and a few uniformed hostesses walking briskly, probably getting ready to board.

The PA system announced something in Flemish about Flight 674, and then repeated it in what was probably Dutch, and finally I heard, "Visitors awaiting Flight 674 from London are requested to contact the information counter."

That was Anju's flight. Suddenly, I had an empty feeling in the pit of my stomach, a premonition of disaster. I moved towards the information counter when I saw the agent coming towards me.

"Mr. Sood," he said, "I think we need a drink."

He must be sensing my anxiety, I thought.

"I'm sorry, Mr. Sood." He put his hand on my shoulder. "The flight from London went down in the English Channel. Rescue operations are in progress. I ... I will keep you informed." He paused. "Mr. Sood, Mr. Sood ..."

June 1975 onwards, Delhi, India
Part One

1

I was disgusted and annoyed. For one thing, it was extremely hot; the temperature hung several degrees above normal, to quote the papers, and then there was this fly pestering me, perching on my hands, cheeks, and arms. At the moment it sat on my pillow rubbing its antennae, in what I could only decipher as glee.

"Well, sir, I think your end is near," I commented.

I picked up a book and cautiously brought it down on target, or so I thought. The breeze thus produced touched me on the shoulder, a conspiratorial touch that was nevertheless fleetingly pleasant. The moment I upturned the book, my feeling of achievement faded; the book's cover was as clean as ever. No spot of orange blood mixed with yellow ochre fluid marred its appearance. Even the pillow was deserted.

"Lucky little creature," I mused. "One moment it's here under this antiquated slow-moving fan, and the next, who knows, maybe in an air-conditioned room. If I were a fly, I would leave this horrible sticky place and seek refuge at Micky's place. Lucky guy, Mukesh, or Micky to friends – has a big room to himself and a cooler – a cooler, the invention of modern science that removes stickiness, perspiration, and restlessness."

I could be indecisive at times. I wanted to go over to Micky's, but that meant ten minutes of brisk cycling down the dusty, hot, deserted roads. My room was not that bad with the record player with stereo output, posters and a bookcase full of comics, books, and magazines. I glanced up at the ceiling. The blades of the fan chopped the air, creating a faint breeze. I thought of Micky sitting in front of his room cooler eating potato chips and reading comics. That did it.

I hurriedly dressed, putting on a striped full-sleeved shirt, blue-gray trousers, and open toe sandals. I wore no belt or socks, knowing that I was not much to look at anyway, and did not mind living up to the reputation.

"I'll be back in a couple of hours," I yelled to my mom, who was further perspiring in the kitchen, and I stepped outdoors with the bicycle key dangling in my hand. Soon, I would be in the comfort of a Cool Home appliance, "the perfect home Climatizer," as the man on the radio advertised. "Low consumption, long lasting, Cool Home really cools your home. Ting."

Once out on the road, I looked around, hoping to see people. I did, but they were a few beggars scattered under large shade trees, like so many wilted flowers. I pedalled faster.

It was not eleven o'clock, but the pavement and road were exuding heat waves. There was no one even in the local market place that I cycled through! I did not pause, for I was already wet with perspiration and wanted to reach Micky's as quickly as possible.

I turned the last corner, and there it was – a three-storey house with pink and grey walls, a veranda on the ground floor and spacious balconies on the two upper floors. My hands tightened on the brakes as I jumped off the bike just outside the gate. A drop of perspiration rolled across my glasses, blurring my field of vision, as I locked the bicycle and hastily made my way to the top floor. Micky and his mother lived here.

The sound of the bell brought a pair of feet to the door.

"Yes?" demanded Micky as he opened the door. "What are you doing here at this time of the day?" he greeted me. "Aren't you hot? Don't you have any sense, visiting people in this heat? Don't you ...?"

"Damn it, let me in," I interrupted impatiently; not angrily, because I knew Micky too well. We had been classmates for almost ten years, and he had a habit of shedding civility around his friends, particularly when his mother was nowhere in the vicinity.

"Ah, yes." He suddenly realised. "Yes, yes, certainly."

I closed the door behind me. "Let's go to your room."

"Are you here to stay?" He eyed me with hands on his waist.

"Well, that's what I had in mind."

"Oh, shit! Okay. But, you don't want a drink, do you? No, you don't. Good. Let me show you my new LP, 'Rock Your Baby'."

I followed him to *cool* pleasure.

"Nobody home?" I asked.

"Well, I'm here."

"What were you doing?"

"Is that any of your business?" he asked slowly, stressing each word, in a tone that implied that I was trespassing his privacy.

"Okay, what do you intend doing now that I am here?"

"Um ... well, I'm gonna play chess. You may, of course, join me. Do I hear any objections?"

He raised his left eyebrow as he spoke, which did not detract from his good looks. He was a handsome boy of sixteen, soon to be seventeen, with an exiguous line of hair above his upper lip. This informal and slightly impertinent behaviour of his was quite normal with me.

"No," I replied. I had no choice, anyway, and I liked chess.

We laid the chessboard on the small round coffee table and squatted cross-legged on chairs opposite each other. Micky did so comfortably, for he was wearing shorts. I was not so comfortable, thanks to my tight-fitting trousers.

"Your move, damn you." His voice echoed in the room.

I moved a pawn. I must admit that seeing him so comfortable made me a bit jealous. First, he was not wearing long trousers, and secondly he was not wearing a shirt. It was a bit unusual, but making mention of it would set off an unnecessary argument; to date, no one had ever won an argument with Micky.

He was quiet through the first few moves, a rare thing, for he hardly ever kept his mouth shut. I heard rumours that he even talked in his sleep!

"Pawn, Queen Four," he said, whatever that meant.

"Check," I retorted, moving a bishop, the only one left.

"Huh?" muttered a perturbed Micky, and I patted my hair, making no attempt to conceal my satisfaction. That was only momentary, for soon I caught his feelings.

"There," he guffawed. "There goes your other bishop. Checkmate, huh? Ha, ha, Vicky baby, you can't beat me when it comes to chess. You know that, 'cause I am the greatest in the field. Ha, ha."

"My foot, you are. My left toe," I replied, showing him the tip of my sandal, which he completely ignored. "Anyway, we'll see who the winner is. We haven't finished yet. Greatest, ha."

"Yeah? We'll surely, definitely and certainly ..."

"See?" I interrupted.

"Yes." Curtness returned. "But, anyway your ..."

His comment was drowned within a loud sound of metal striking plaster, followed by wood striking solid rubber, ending in metal striking plaster again. I almost fell off my chair, and in the process I overturned the chessboard. It was an accident, but nevertheless, a favourable happening for me.

We will have to begin all over again, I thought, *and I just might win the game.*

I blessed my long, gangling limbs which had a habit of getting in everyone's and everything's way, usually resulting in messing up something or the other. I did not really mind these gifts from God, but the curses and 'be-carefuls' that usually followed like a well worn gramophone record, sometimes made me curse them. What had just happened was only an example of the problem. In jumping up hastily, my long legs somehow got stuck under the table and ... well ... I am clumsy and I do not like admitting the fact.

Micky looked in the direction of the sound, the door to his room, his face an expression of calm acceptance. Instinctively, my eyes drifted towards the source of his attention where another wonder awaited me. Framed in the doorway was the figure of a girl!

Oh God, I thought, *what is this world coming to? Even the quiet demeanour of girls seemed to be changing to aggression! What's going to happen next?*

"Oh, I am sorry, very sorry," she said from the doorway.

"Not at all," Micky replied.

I remained quiet. It was not in my nature to talk to strangers, particularly if the stranger also happened to be a girl.

It dawned on me that Micky was quite accustomed to this. She had literally kicked the door open and gate-crashed our privacy. It seemed my presence reminded her of her manners, so she blurted an apology. I knew she was unaware that Micky had a guest; nevertheless, it was not quite appropriate to barge into his room without permission or advance notice, or even a knock! What if he had been changing his clothes? Not that he was fully dressed even now, but still ...

"Hey, Mukesh, may I have a word with you?" asked our visitor.

"Yeah, spit it."

He needs to learn some manners, I thought. *This was no way to speak to a girl!*

"I wish to spit in private," she responded contemptuously.

"No secrets in public. Start talking or get lost. Can't you see I am busy?"

I wondered whether I would ever be able to converse with a girl that way.

"Vicky, you clumsy idiot," Micky exclaimed, shifting his attention to me.

Doesn't he spare anyone? I wondered. *Insulting me in front of a girl! I'll kill him.*

"Set up that damned board again. You don't play fair."

Enough was enough, but I dared not rebel; it was not easy in the presence of a girl.

"Just because you were losing, you had to ..."

"You gonna come out here or ....?" She left the sentence dangling.

I admired her guts. I regarded her carefully. She was quite good-looking. You could not call her beautiful in the true sense of the word, but dressed in black trousers and a yellow T-shirt, she looked smart and cute.

Micky gave up with a shrug, and went outside in the balcony.

"Yes," I heard him say.

As they talked, I stole an occasional look at her. I could not help myself, and I did not quite understand it. She seemed a decent girl, graceful and gentle. She had a soft, musical voice. I could not make out the words, but the general tone was sweet, punctuated now and then with melodious giggles. She was pretty when she laughed, and about my age – around fifteen – not too tall, with a simple, attractive ponytail for a hairstyle. She made a real pleasing appearance.

It was not my nature to go around admiring girls, but ... well, I am human, and there had to be a first time. I had never before had this feeling which was hard to describe; but my heart was thumping in the most unaccountable way. I had often heard that every boy has a girl in his dreams and every girl a boy. I never had as yet, but she looked really terrific.

"Okay, Micksie, I'd better leave before your friend starts cursing me. Be a good boy, okay?" she admonished.

Why would I curse her? I mused. *What wrong had she done me?*

"Okay, okay, vanish, vamoose, scoot, disappear, get lost," concluded our dear diplomatic Micky.

He shouldn't be so rude, I thought, *but who would tell him? Not I, for sure.*

"And here's a kiss for you, sweetie. Ummm ..." she responded.

As soon as her footsteps faded away, I collared Micky, pulled him aside, and sat him down on the bed.

"Hey," he growled," are you out of your mind?"

"No," I said hastily, "but you're going to answer some questions for me, and no funny business."

He was clearly amazed. "Ay, ay, sir. Sure," he replied, proceeding to make himself comfortable by placing a pillow in his lap and crossing his arms on it. A stupid grin replaced his former expression.

"Why aren't you ever serious, damn you?" I paused for a moment. "Is that girl a friend of yours?"

"Yes," he responded.

I think he anticipated what was coming next, for suddenly he started fishing in his pocket.

"I mean in that sense, you know." I had to confirm, because in the past I noticed that Micky developed a crush on every girl who even reciprocated his casual glance. "I hope you understand what I mean ..."

"Well, I most certainly do, and the answer is ..." he paused as he fished out a handkerchief from his pocket and blew his nose in it.

"Go ahead, dammit, torture me. Every dog has his day. Someday you'll need me, and then I shall seek revenge."

"No," he announced, and a thrill rushed through me, a new kind of feeling.

"Good," I replied, and hastened to discuss the innermost subject of my heart. "Who is she? Where does she live? What is her name? Her ..."

"Cool down, cool down, man. Not so fast."

He stood up and rested his hands on his waist. "Why the hell are you so interested?"

"Never mind. Just answer me."

He stared at me intently. “You,” he finally said, pointing at me, "have taken a fancy to her.” He paused, and winked at me. “You have, haven’t you, Vicky?”

“Will you shut up? Please ...”

“My goodness, Vicky,” he gasped. “You? You of all the people? Lost your heart to a girl? Tch, tch.”

“I said answer me, and quit this ... what you call ... oh, forget it. I mean we’ll culminate this stupid talk of yours and go forth with mine.”

“Excitement, excitement,” he jeered with a coy smile. “Hey, admit it, buddy. I’ll be a great help to you, I promise.”

“I said ...”

“Your slightest wish is my command, sir,” he said calmly. “Now, one by one, let’s see ... She’s fourteen, nearly fifteen, five foot one, will be studying in our school after these holidays, in grade nine, and goes by the name of Anju. Satisfied? Anything else?”

I opened my mouth to speak, but he waved his hand and continued, “Her father is a doctor in the army, and was recently transferred here from Bombay.”

“Come on, Micky, don’t be so curt. It’s just that ... well, I was furious because you did not introduce her.”

“Why should I have introduced her to you? You don’t like girls, remember?” He scratched his head, reminding me of a certain mammal I saw at the zoo.

"N ... not really, but ... um ..."

"Do you want to know her?"

"Yeah. Could you ... I mean, would she be willing to ... I mean, be a friend?"

"Well, I can try."

"I'll give you a treat. Whatever you say, wherever you say. Please ..." I begged.

"Look, Vicky, you've got lots of books and she's a bookworm. Why don't you start by lending her books? I can be a go-between and help you get acquainted, then you can take it from there."

"Okay, go ahead."

2

It was just ten in the morning and I was already at Micky's. Actually, I had gone over to pick up my trigonometry book, which Micky had borrowed, and forgotten to return. Summer holidays were about to end, and I had not quite finished my holiday assignments, nor had Micky for that matter.

After I got the book, and had a nice little chat with him, he decided to return to the algebra problems he was working on.

"Hey, Vicky," he called out as I got near the door. "If you have the time, would you please help me with a few of these algebra things?"

I readily agreed. It was a legitimate excuse for me to spend time at his place, and wait for Anju to show up.

"Why don't you come over and get some comics today?" I suggested, pulling a chair close to the bed, where Micky's books were sprawled out. Someone's cute face was playing on my mind as I uttered the suggestion.

"Algebra first," said Micky. "Question nine."

While we were working on the third problem, a soft knock came at the door.

"Yeah," called out Micky, and Anju appeared, wearing a pair of orange flared trousers and Bata bathroom slippers. I quickly looked down, pretending to concentrate on math. Actually, I was nervous and excited. Water welled up in my eyes and I could feel my ears grow red.

"Micky," she said, "your mom is at our place, and she asked me to tell you two that there's a Laurel and Hardy movie on TV in five minutes. You can come to watch it if you want."

"Coming," said the ever-ready-to-stop-studying Micky, and hurriedly closed his books. "Let's go, Vicky."

She walked out the door. I could sense her absence without looking.

"I ... I'm not coming."

"What the hell?"

"I ... I ... I'll just get nervous. You know how it is," I stammered as he started dragging me. "Why don't you buy a TV set if you are so interested?"

"Will you finance it? My mom does not have the money."

A few taps on the door were followed by Anju's irritated voice, "You coming or not?"

Now's my chance, I thought.

"On one condition," I whispered. "An introduction."

As we stepped out and came face to face with Anju, he began, "Anju, meet my friend, Victor Sood. Vicky, this is Anju."

I had been planning the occasion for a long time and thought I would shake her hand.

Now she was here, and I could not even look directly at her, let alone move my hands! We exchanged hellos and proceeded to her place, one floor below.

I did not laugh during the entire movie, being afraid that I might not sound charming, or my lips might not part gracefully. I confined myself to smiling once when it was really funny. I did not even turn my eyes in her direction, but my ears repeatedly caught her sweet, melodious giggles and those were real satisfying moments.

"I'll be moving along," I said after the movie ended. I picked up my trigonometry book.

"Why don't you come over every day, Vicky," Micky's mom invited, "and help this fashion-centred son of mine with his holiday assignments?"

I accepted the invitation, an offer I could not refuse – a chance to see *her* daily.

I opened my book case.

"I'd like a Harold Robbins' book," Micky said, as he started pawing through my well-arranged library.

"Nothing doing," I exclaimed, going to the rescue of my books.

"Okay, okay. Hey, you've got *Dracula* and *The Godfather*!"

"So?" I was cool. "Look, Micky, you aren't getting anything except the seven comics, so stop exclaiming. "You may read them before you pass them on," I added as an afterthought.

He refused to listen. "I want to read that horny scene in *The Godfather*, where Sonny Corleone's brother, you know, screws ..."

"Here." I handed over a bunch of comics to him. "Don't tell her that I ... well ... I mean, that I directed you to pass them on."

He faced me with a stupid grin.

"Damn you, why aren't you ever serious?"

"Hey, Vicky, what's the matter? Don't be so damned gloomy. You know ... you know what this means, eh?" he said, shaking his head like it was balanced on a wedge.

I remained quiet. It seemed the wisest thing to do, considering the circumstances.

"You're in love," he announced, with a flourish.

"Okay, okay, shut up," I said. "Want a Coke?"

"You treating?"

"May I even dare expect otherwise?"

We went to the corner store and had chilled Cokes. I did not wish to admit feelings for Anju openly; I knew Micky a bit too well. If he knew something, it was inevitable that everyone he was even remotely acquainted with, would soon be a party to it, too. He also loved taking advantage of everything and everyone. Telling him that he was a wicked bastard would be inviting trouble, and at the moment he was my only link with Anju.

"Tell you what, Micky, I'll come over to your place tomorrow evening with more comics. Okay?"

He nodded, and I added, "You can return me these at that time."

3

I shut my books. I had been studying all morning and afternoon, trying to catch up on my assignments. It was evening, and I faced a decision. Should I, or should I not go over to Micky's? I would love to see Anju again. There was no reason for me to hesitate or procrastinate. I ought to go since I had told Micky I would, but the clock ticked a hundred and twenty times before I made up my mind.

I put on my new shirt and trousers and dabbed some cologne on my collar. My hair was too long, I needed better frames for my glasses, and my teeth were in need of attention; I doubted I looked very attractive. Anyway, it was me, the natural me, the usual me. I always tried to make myself believe that there was no point trying to impress someone with false glittering. When I tried, I never succeeded, but this time I was determined not to even try. If Anju wanted to befriend me, it would be with the real me.

At seven o'clock I was on my bike pedalling towards Micky's. My dad had a scooter, but I was not permitted to use it as I was only fifteen, and could not get a driver's license.

It was a beautiful trip, and my heart was completely enveloped in happy thoughts. I was thinking positively. It had rained an hour earlier, and the air was still damp, but pleasant. Saturday evenings are the times best suited for such feelings. The streets bustled with activity. It was not yet dark, but neon signs glittered and teenagers walked casually about in the streets. Who would not have appreciated an evening walk in such pleasant weather? Cars rushed past and honked when I got in their way, but I did not avoid them; instead, I irritated the drivers by cycling in the middle of the road. There was joviality, cheerfulness, and gladness everywhere. Even water drops on the leaves of the trees were in harmony with the season, and glittered happily in the fading light.

At the zenith, the clouds gathered around the setting sun were tinged orange – a figurative colour, signifying warmth, happiness, and love. It seemed as if the heavens were celebrating the arrival of the monsoons. I could sense the fullness of their bliss, and my heart was filled with 'orange' feeling. I felt a change taking place in me, the transformation from a loner to a gregarious person. It was the first time that I had ever desired the company of a girl.

To reach Micky's place I had to turn six corners. As I turned the last one, I saw her. She was standing in front of her house, resting against a Fiat, which I presumed to be theirs and which it turned out to be, talking to two girls who were probably her friends. I glanced at her quickly; two ponytails, a rosy face, a yellow printed frock, bare legs, and Bata bathroom slippers. To reach Micky's floor I had to pass her, and that posed a problem – the two steps at the gate. With her so close there could be a mishap. I might slip, nervous as I was, so as I passed her I looked the other way, and reached Micky's room unharmed, externally, anyway.

"Hey, what happened? Why are you so breathless?" queried Micky as he let me in.

I waved my hand and shook my head.

"Did you encounter her on the way? Did she say anything?" pursued Micky. "You're a damn punctual fellow, not a minute late – seven fifteen sharp. Wow!"

I sat down on his bed and wiped my forehead.

"I think a drink would do you good," Micky suggested. "What'll you have, squash or Rooh-af-za?"

"Nothing yet, thank you," I replied, trying to regain my composure.

Micky sounded genuinely surprised, "Why are you so formal?"

"Damn it, you good-for-nothing toad, you know I am trying to be impressive. I've gotta be a paragon of good manners."

"Okay, okay," he said understandingly. "She's not here yet."

"How do you know she won't appear without notice? I have to remain alert."

"Yeah," he agreed. "Now?"

"Have you talked to her?"

"A number of times, yes." He picked up his pen and started chewing on it.

"I mean, about me." I wanted to shout, but I had to be patient.

"No," was his short reply. I glanced at him questioningly, which prompted him to add, "I didn't get a chance."

"Micky," I said, looking directly at him, "don't act like a fool, because you and I know very well that no one can be more discreet than you when you choose to be." I paused. "So damn you, choose to be discreet. Now, listen to me, and advise me without being so high-handed. You know that I like her a lot. I ... I ..."

"So what are you to do?" He completed my sentence. "Hmm, well." He started munching on his pen. "Hmm. Listen, man, don't get so damned excited. I'll do something for you."

"When? When?"

"Soon."

"Please do it without letting her know."

"Don't worry," he answered, patting my shoulder.

"I ... I ... well, I ... Dammit," I cursed under my breath, "this will lead me nowhere."

"What's wrong?" Micky asked, scanning me.

"Sh ... sh ... she ... she's here. B ... be ... behind you ... outside," I whispered, my voice hoarse and shaky.

"Oh, really," exclaimed Micky, jumping off his bed to greet her. She was still outside, talking to his mother. "Come," he said and dragged me to her.

I felt sweaty all over. I do not know whether it was the heat or nervousness. I knew I was drenched in my own perspiration and my legs were so shaky I had to hold onto the balcony railing to keep myself upright.

She looked at me, and I looked at her. I must have looked ridiculous. I felt like a coward, nervous and self-conscious to a heartbreaking degree.

"Hi," greeted Micky.

"Hi, Chweetie," came the prompt reply.

She looked at me again. When she moved her lips to speak, I felt the blood rush to my cheek, as my heart beat faster and louder. It was a wonder no one heard it. I was on the verge of dropping the comics in my hand; the other hand clung to the railing.

"Here," I said, thrusting the comics at her, only to have them pushed aside by Micky who inconsiderately inserted himself between us.

"Vicky," he said imperiously, "what's all this nonsense? Either you sit down inside and let me do the talking, or you talk and I'll go sit inside. Your ardour is showing. Go inside."

I nodded and walked back inside. *The bastard! Imagine, insulting me in front of her again! What was I supposed to be? His servant, the way he ordered me to 'Go inside'?*

"You shouldn't be so hard on your friend, Micky," I heard her say. "After all, he's lending you so many comics, and as you say, he's crazy about ..."

"He's a bum."

The nerve! My first instinct was to bash him, but the feeling that I had made a fool of myself stayed me. I felt so ashamed that I vowed to befriend Anju or perish in the attempt. I suffered agonies no one suspected, and my heart beat as painfully as a recruit under fire for the first time.

"Yeah, why are you here? I mean why do you have this habit of dropping in whenever Vicky is here?" He looked at me. "Any ...?"

"No, no, no. No sentimental reasons," she said, and smiled.

"Cut the smile," Micky clipped. "Hurry up. What do you want? Mama's in the kitchen, if you want something."

"I came over for more comics."

"And pray, how did you know that a fresh supply of comics was here? Do you have a crystal ball or something?" A wide smile accompanied his remark.

"Well, I saw your friend coming with comics in his hands, so I thought ..."

"Vicky," called out Micky, "she was on the lookout for you."

"Wh ... wha ... whadda ... what do you mean?" I blurted and saw her pulling Micky's ears when I looked up. My God! Such guts! Suddenly I was glad that I was not outside. Who knows – she might have done that to me!

"Micky stop fooling around and hand over those comics," she said giggling. "If you don't want to lend them to me, I'll talk to your friend directly."

I suddenly felt like going to the bathroom, the only place where she would not follow me.

"Learn to behave like a gentleman," I heard her say when I came back. She was trying to snatch the comics from Micky, but he was too tall for her. I saw her jump to reach for them, pull his collar, and bang her fist into his stomach. My legs gave way, and I sat down.

"Okay," she said, giving up. "You're not going to give them to me, eh? Let your friend go. I'll turn that bloody smile of yours into a scowl. Good-bye."

As she turned to leave, I got up hastily and accidentally overturned the table. The noise attracted her attention, and she paused to stare at me. Her expression was not one of surprise or disapproval or censure or horror or anything I had expected; it was just a peculiar, undecipherable expression that lasted a second before changing to a smile and laughter. I was embarrassed, but hid it, as I joined in the laughter.

"Clown," she muttered, stepping towards the stairs.

"Wait a second," I blurted, hurrying to the door and tripping over my own shoelaces. I fell headlong out the doorway. I do not remember whether it hurt or not, but as soon as I was on my feet again, I snatched the comics from Micky, and handed them to Anju. "Here, Miss .... er ...er ..."

"Anju," she announced, tilting her head. "And you, Master ... er ... er ..."

Clearly she was mimicking me. How could a girl be so candid? Weren't they supposed to be discreet and coy, and look down when talking to boys, or not talk to strangers at all?

And then, it happened again. "I ... I ... I'm ..."

"Good-bye, Anju," broke in Micky. " I suggest you leave. You have the comics, and you've troubled him enough. Disappear, vanish ..."

I trembled uncontrollably. The agitation that I had felt earlier over Micky's unpardonable conduct disturbed me again, as he repeated his unkindness. Why start hinting and suggesting when a good relationship was developing?

"Humph," she retorted curtly. "Good-bye, Micky." She left with a "Damn it."

I was exasperated at Micky's behaviour but did not say anything, because if I had, and he was offended, it might affect our friendship, and I would have to give up my visits to his house, which would mean good-bye to Anju. The thought was unbearable. I descended the stairs without looking at Micky.

4

I could not restrain myself from going over to Micky's again. I admit that I am rather weak-willed. I am not sure whether I had done the right thing. Probably not, for this time Anju became furious.

As was my custom, I began the sacred rites of preparation at six o'clock, and at seven, I was at Micky's locking my bike. Anju was not around, so I went upstairs with a cool, calm mind. I had been thinking over the happenings of the day before and reached the conclusion that it was time Micky got a firing from me. His mom told me he was somewhere downstairs, and said I could wait if I wanted to. I pulled an easy chair out on the balcony and got comfortable.

Presently, Micky made his appearance. There was a Sikh with him, whom he introduced as Ginny, a friend of his. I got up, shook hands with Ginny, and offered him my seat which he politely declined.

"Today we had solid fun," Micky said, rubbing his hands together. "This guy borrowed his dad's car, and we drove slowly behind a couple of girls near ..."

"My comics?" I cut in, looking at him matter-of-factly.

"She still has them," he responded. He walked to the railing and stood resting his back against it. "You know, Ginny, this guy is after Anju. He desperately ..."

Enough is enough, and this was going too far, taking liberties with my affairs. What did he mean telling every Tom, Dick and Harry about Anju and me? Suddenly, I recalled my resolution.

"Micky," I shouted.

It had no effect on him. He continued relating to Ginny all that I had been doing.

"Micky, you goddamned bloody, stinking, good-for-nothing, impetuous idiot, will you shut up?"

He shifted his attention to me. The look of surprise on his face seemed genuine enough. It was uncommon for me to verbally abuse anyone.

"What the hell do you mean publicizing my affairs? I will not stand for it. I ... I ..." I was breathless.

"Finished?" he asked coolly putting his foot up on the railing to tighten his shoelace. That frustrated me even more.

"Trying to be calm, and er ... er ..."

"Nonchalant is the word, sweetheart," he finished, putting his foot down. "Isn't it?"

"You're hopeless, Micky, absolutely hopeless." I was thoroughly disgusted. "Why do you do such things? Why? Why did you send her away just when I was about to get a break? Why do you spread all the canards? Why, Micky, why?"

"Cool down, man, cool down," he replied, grinning. "Now if you don't want to sit down, may I?"

I could see that he was not going to accept the fact that he had done something mean. Even if he did, he was not going to repent. The way he was grinning was immature and childish, not at all compatible with sixteen.

"I know one thing for sure, Mr. Mukesh," I said icily. "You're not a friend. You don't want me to be happy. You just want to appear superior to others, and since I permit it, you take advantage. You ... where are you going? I'm talking to you, Micky. Micky?"

He left, just walked away while I talked. Ginny stood looking off the balcony. He turned with a stupid grin on his face as I stopped shouting.

"Where's Micky?" he asked.

"Went inside."

"Vicky," Micky said, as he returned, "don't be so damned angry. I'll explain to you why I sent her away. You don't want me to tell Ginny anything about this?"

I shook my head.

"Okay, I won't." He sounded sorry, but he was not genuinely repenting, for that was not in his nature. However, softer words did cushion some of the tension. "Here," he continued, "have a Coke."

"No."

"Let's forget the incident. Look, you're my friend, and I will help you. You want her, you'll get her. Faithful admirers like you are rare. I'll do my best for you."

He picked up the Coke bottle and offered it to me again. "Please."

"Wait till I tell the gang," Ginny blurted and burst out laughing. "Particularly, Anju."

I stared helplessly at Micky.

"He's just teasing," Micky said. "He won't do anything of the sort."

Yelling had hurt my parched throat, so I accepted the Coke, albeit with a show of reluctance. I took one sip and asked, "Your reasons?"

Micky ignored my question and turned to Ginny. "Care for a walk?"

Ginny nodded, and I repeated my question. Micky signalled, "After he leaves," meaning Ginny. We gulped down our Cokes, left the bottles on the chair, and started towards the stairs.

Halfway down, Micky changed his mind. "Why not go for a bike ride instead? We've had a car ride, and scooter ride, so why not have a bicycle ride?"

No one objected. Micky took the key from me – the bike was unlocked – and rolled it out of the gate. Now, after all, Micky was Micky. He made so much noise rolling it out that a middle-aged woman, presumably Anju's mother, came out to tell him that Anju was not home. With Ginny riding pillion on the carrier, and me on the bar in front, Micky started pedalling.

The sun had already set, and the world was gradually getting enveloped in darkness. As we rounded the first corner, Micky braked, realizing there was a power failure. There were no electric lights in the streets or in the houses and shops that lined them. I was fearful – darkness always frightens me. There was hardly enough light to see, but Micky continued to pedal. Ginny somehow sensed my fright and produced a mini-torch from his pocket which he handed to me. I thanked him and accepted it.

We rode around the local market for a while, and then His Lordship granted my prayers. We saw Anju entering a confectionery shop, and suddenly all of us felt thirsty. Micky proposed that we have another Coke, Ginny seconded it and I had no choice, though it was also proposed that I would pay for all of us.

"Three Cokes," I told the man at the counter.

"No, five," corrected Micky, nudging me. "Dammit, look to your right."

I had been consciously avoiding looking that side because I knew Anju and one of her friends was inspecting something in the light of a candle.

"Today's your opportunity," whispered Micky. "Treat them to Cokes, too. That way you'll get to spend time with them, and you can get acquainted."

He must have seen the confused expression on my face, for he suggested that he act as the host and offer them drinks.

"Hey, wait," Micky called out to Anju as she passed us.

"Oh, hi!" she said. "I see you guys are having Cokes. Well ... um, it wouldn't be gentlemanly if you did not offer us some. We may not accept, but you might at least offer."

"We've already ordered Cokes for you," replied Micky.

"This is a dream! It is simply not possible," said Anju, amazed as Micky gave the two girls a bottle each. "Micky acting so generous? Something's fishy." She looked at the bottle for a second and said, "You're not paying, are you?"

"Why don't you just drink it and vanish? Look what you've done. You've been talking to me, and Svati has been talking to Ginny, but nobody has noticed our host." He pointed at me as he gulped down the rest of his Coke.

"Oh, so that's it. And pray, why is he treating me and Svati?"

"Ask him."

I was getting cold feet. The dreaded moment had arrived.

"Yeah." Anju turned towards me. "Why are you buying me a drink? You don't know me that well, do you? No, you don't. Then why? Eh?"

"I ... I ... I ..." I took a step backward and bumped into a girl standing behind me. "Oh, I'm sorry," I apologized, as Micky came to my rescue.

"It was my idea." To me, he said, "Let's go outside, it's getting a bit hot in here."

I gladly followed him out, and as I was unlocking the bike, Anju came out and hurled a "Thanks" at me. So did Svati. The man at the counter gave me an amused smile.

A few minutes later, as we were returning to Micky's place, we encountered Anju and Svati again. As soon as Micky saw them, he stopped the bike, told Ginny and me to exchange seats, and took the torch from me. I could not figure what he was doing. When I asked, he said, "Wait and see."

Fine, I thought, *I'll wait and see.*

He began what was clearly eve-teasing, something I had never done or participated in before. First, Ginny encircled the girls with the light from the torch, moving it up and down and finally focussing it on their legs. They turned around, and the beam shifted to their eyes, blinding them. As they raised their hands to cover their eyes, Ginny shifted the beam to Anju's chest. I did not wish to get involved in such activities, especially with Anju. As Ginny shifted the beam to their eyes again, Micky started riding the bike around them, ringing the bell loudly. I jumped off the bike.

I won't let Micky ruin any good impression I may have made on Anju, I thought. I walked the rest of the way back to Micky's house.

"Where did you vanish to, damn you?" demanded Micky when he found me waiting for him in his room. "We had a lot of fun after you left. Anju started crying, and Svati ..."

"The reasons?" I cut in.

"You're a bloody idiot!" He kicked the door shut. "You made a fool of yourself again. What the hell is wrong with you? Why do you lose your balance when she talks to you? Your ardour and nervousness are too damn obvious. I could see she sensed your idiosyncrasy and was tempted to rag you further. If I hadn't sent her away, she would have enjoyed herself thoroughly .... then she would have calumniated and ... dammit, you can understand the rest."

"I ... I'm ..."

He gestured me to stop. "You fall at her feet and you get nothing. Learn to be elusive, hard-to-catch."

He's right, I thought. *Why the hell am I bringing comics for her every day and treating her to Cokes when I don't even know her feelings? The way she thanked me was more like a slap.*

Micky selected a record and put it on the player. As he put the stylus on it, he turned and asked icily, “Satisfied?”

“Fine,” I replied sheepishly and walked up to him. “Micky, would you please do something for me?”

He nodded.

“I would like to have my comics back, yesterday’s and today’s, which are at Miss Anju’s. Get them, please.”

“What ?” He was exasperated. “Why the hell do you want to ruin the good impression you’ve created?”

“What impression?” I retorted. “You just...”

“The one that I have been trying to help you build.”

“Have you?” I said mockingly. “Look, it’s getting late and I have to go. I want my comics immediately, and Mr. Mukesh, you know that when I say something, I mean it.”

“She hasn’t read them yet. You’ll get them when you come over tomorrow.”

“I am waiting, Mr. Micky,” I said stubbornly.

“Wait near your bike,” he said and left the room. “Crazy idiot,” I heard him muttering.

As soon as Micky was out of sight, I realized that I had acted like a fool. Okay, I wanted revenge because she had ragged me, mocked me, whatever. Why? Was it because I suffered from an inferiority complex? Teasing was her nature, but who do you normally tease? Only the people you like. Maybe she did like me, as Micky had just hinted. I could see it in her eyes the other day when I gave her the comics. Had I not been the one at whose request this give-but-no-take business had taken shape? No, I would not take them back until she had read them.

"Here," Micky's voice interrupted my train of thought. "Here are six of them – yesterday's. The other two plus today's eight, she refuses to return, says you'll understand, which you don't." He paused for breath. "If you persist, she said, she might let you have them."

"No, no," I exclaimed. "Let her take her time, there's no hurry."

"Really, Vicky." His tone was nonplussed and disgusted. "You're a salt and pepper mixture. One moment ..."

The door opposite me opened and Svati stepped out.

"I'd better leave now," I said. "It's getting late, and I don't like to ride in the dark."

5

I resumed my seat."Try this one," I said, pointing out the problem to Micky with my finger on the cyclostyled sheet. "I've been trying to solve it for quite some time now, unsuccessfully. Why don't you try it? You might succeed. Meanwhile, I'll try problem six, okay?"

"Ay, ay," he replied, offhandedly.

As his mother pointed out, he was not the least bit interested in studies, particularly mathematics.

"Hey, you know something?" I nudged him.

He did not respond, so I chewed on a pen halfway in *my* mouth. His attitude perplexed me, but I continued, "I brought four love stories today, along with two Harvey comics, and," I continued excitedly, "and I put the lyrics of the song 'I Think I Love You' in one of them. What do you think she will do when she discovers them?"

Silence.

"Have I done the right thing? Huh? Are you listening?"

"She doesn't read love stories," he replied indifferently and continued working.

"How do you know?" I placed my pen on the table. I was fuming. "I ..."

"Vicky, this has to stop. Are you here to study or pester me about Anju?" He jabbed his pen at the table but stopped just in time to save the nib from being damaged. "Look, you may not be serious about studies, but I am." He stressed the last two words. "I suggest we forget Anju for a while and concentrate on mathematics."

"I ... I didn't mean to," I stammered, picking up my pen. But, something popped up again as I was scrutinizing a problem. "Hey, Micky, look. What a coincidence. It says here to take a line AX and cut AK equal to fourteen point five centimetres. Ha! AK and fourteen and a half ..." I smiled and looked at Micky, then my smile vanished.

"There you go again!" he shouted, slamming his book shut. "I'll tell you what. I'm gonna call her up right now and you can chat with her to your heart's content." He sounded like he meant it.

I wondered what had irritated him.

"Anju!" Micky's voice resonated throughout the building.

"No! Come on, Micky, stop that," I pleaded trying to pull him back into the room.

He clung to the door of his room. "Look, you've been jabbering about her ever since you first saw her, though she's not that great looking or cute," he said with a now-you'll-have-your-wish-granted expression. "You've repeatedly expressed your desire for a tete-a-tete with her. Fine, you will have your wish." He was merciless. "Anju!"

"I can't. Look, why do you want me to make a fool of myself? Please, man, don't," I pleaded as I tried to pull him back from the balcony where he now clung to the railing, but he was at least twenty pounds heavier than me, and I had no luck. In the process, I turned around and noticed we had a visitor.

A stranger stood in the doorway. She was tall, about five feet six, clad in faded jeans and a round necked horizontally striped T-shirt, together with shoulder length hair parted twice so that the central portion covered the forehead and the rest framed her face, covering part of either shoulder. She was beautiful, and looked dignified even in that casual outfit. I figured her to be around eighteen. It was not Anju, who evidently had not heard Micky. Micky did not pursue calling her. I was thankful.

"Hi, Alka," Micky welcomed the visitor, ushering her into the room.

"Anju told me that you'd be going to the British Council Library today," she stated, looking around as if searching for something.

"I might. Why?"

"Would you take my books along, if you go?"

"Yeah, sure," he agreed. Then, "Uh ... oh." He seemed to realize something. "I forgot to introduce you. Alka, this is Victor, my classmate. Vicky, this is Alka, Anju's older sister."

She stretched out her hand, which I hesitantly accepted.

"How do you do?" I managed to say.

"How do you do?" she replied.

That was all. Alka turned to Micky and asked him for the comics I had brought. He gave them to her, and without a word of thanks, she started for the door. As she was about to descend the stairs, Micky called to her.

"Hey, Alka, we've been working with some unsolvable math problems. Do you think you could give us a hand?"

"Well, maybe. I have several things I need to be doing, but I'll take a look at them."

"Which one?" she asked sitting down on Micky's chair.

"Number five. I think it's a misprint, because it's not possible to construct the triangle if you're not given angle B. We have tried it several times, but haven't been successful. See if you can figure out something."

She started fidgeting with her T-shirt button. "Hmm." She opened it. "Hmmm." She looked at me, and I gave her my pen and a notebook. She went through the problem again, all the while chewing on my pen. Suddenly, she said, "Micky, why were you calling Anju?"

I suddenly felt sick, scared that he would embarrass me again, and he did.

"Well," he said looking at me, "this friend of mine," he pointed at me, "wanted to ..."

"Excuse me," I interrupted. "May I have a glass of water?"

"Wait a sec, man. Yeah ... he wanted to talk to her." He darted to the kitchen, leaving Alka and me alone.

"You know Anju?" she questioned.

I could feel my ears grow hot and feel the water welling in my eyes.

"Well," I replied, hesitating, "can't say that I do, nor can I say that I don't, but ... well, a little bit, all that I could ..."

"Yeah, all that he could glean from me." Micky completed the sentence, changing the sense altogether. I scowled as he handed me the glass of water. He looked over her shoulder. "Yes, that's how we tried it, too."

She looked at him, then at me, and proceeded to scrutinize the solution. I cursed Micky. Granted that talking about Anju was my favourite pastime, and there was nothing wrong with it. I liked her a lot, but Micky had this habit of disclosing my feelings to everybody and making me look like a fool.

He said, "Now if we take BC as the base and construct angle C, we ..."

My half crazed, my pre-occupied mind again darted to Anju, as her beautiful, innocent child-like face floated in my imagination. I visualized her sitting with a comic in her lap, her large brown eyes looking straight ahead, at nothing in particular, as her mind filled with thoughts of me.

"You were right," I heard Alka say.

The three words jolted my mind back to reality, and I realised that I was hopelessly in love. In my opinion, which is an inspiration from Kim Grove, the author of *Love Is...* love was thinking of her when you should be attending to other business. As Alka's voice floated in the room, I wondered whether love at my age was really possible.

"Yeah," said Micky. "Number nine. Algebra part." He turned the leaf over and pointed out the problem to her. "This one."

I decided to pay attention. After all, I was supposed to be supervising Micky's studies.

"Vicky," I heard Micky say, "she'll be able to crack it. She must have done it when she was in the eleventh grade. Or well, she will apply what she has learned in her first year and half of college in Chandigarh."

"Yeah." I agreed.

"Hmm," murmured Alka as she read the problem and pulled a sheet of paper towards her. Micky was still scrutinizing the solution to the plane geometry problem. "Hmmm."

"Now, if we take this as X," she said, writing it down, "and this as Y." She jotted again. "We'll have this." More calculations.

"Then this is equal to this." I nodded instinctively. "Equating, we get this, right?"

"Yeah," I replied and nodded again. She looked up at me.

"Hey, Micky, what's the answer? Three-fourths and one fourth?"

"No," he replied. "It's eighty-two and eighty-two thirds."

"Hmm." She receded into a muttering spell while she tried again. "There, it's done. You take this equal to this." The pen moved over the paper. "And then you solve these three equations simultaneously." The paper became dirtier. "The answer is X equal to eighty-two." She beamed. "Next? Any more?"

Meanwhile, a figure dressed in brown flared trousers, Bata slippers and a black skivvy had crept quietly into the room and settled unnoticed in a corner. Micky and Alka were engrossed in the math problems, and I was, well, dreaming about Anju. I had no problem admitting the fact, for love is, again inspired by Kim Grove, not letting her slip from your mind ...

I am dressed immaculately and she is looking her most beautiful. I go up to her, take her hands in mine and kiss them. She makes no effort to pull them away.

"Have you seen 'Crazy Boys of the Games', my sweet?" I say.

"No, not yet," she replies.

"Then how about watching it with me?" I invite her.

"Oh, no, I couldn't possibly." She gestures with her hands, indicating helplessness. "I invited Svati, that friend of mine you were teasing the other day, to go with me."

"It wasn't my fault, Anju," I plead obsequiously. "Micky was handling the bike, and Ginny had the torch. Why should I be censured for that distasteful incident?"

She smiles secretly. "Well, I haven't accused you, have I?"

"No, but .... well, I'll tell you what? We'll take Svati with us. Micky can come too, if he wants." I look at her, tender hope in my eyes. "C'mon, say yes, be a good girl. Please, honey?"

"Well ..."

"Oh, thanks, thanks a lot."

She stares at me momentarily, and then smiles coyly.

"I take it that means, yes? I'll get the tickets for the Saturday matinee tomorrow. Would that be okay, Sweets?"

"Well, I don't know. I just ...."

"... came for the comics he brought this morning." A voice shook me out of my reverie. It was Anju, and she was pointing at me.

I was startled. Where did she come from? I suddenly straightened up, and the action lifted the two fore legs of my chair, bringing them down on the floor with a loud bang. The sound of the impact turned all eyes on me.

"What's the matter, Vicky?" Micky glared.

"Huh?" I looked at them blankly. "Oh, oh, nothing. Nothing at all. I ... I ... suppose I was bitten by a mosquito." I tried to grin, unsuccessfully.

Micky understood, and decided to humiliate me further.

"Mosquitoes? Here? At this time of the day?"

"Maybe it was something else," I replied sheepishly, trying to defend myself.

"Mosquitoes, nothing," Micky jeered. "You were startled because Anju was pointing at you." He grinned. "Weren't you, Vicky? You were, weren't you? Oh, you needn't blush. She knows."

They all burst out laughing. To hide my embarrassment, I joined in the laughter.

"Look at Romeo laugh." Micky pointed at me, his face flushed, one hand clutching his belly. "The lover lad laughs ...."

"I haven't all day." Anju cut him off, scowling. "The comics?"

I kicked Micky under the table as a sign to remind him of the love stories. I did not want to be conspicuous.

He understood perfectly. "I know. You don't need to kick me under the table."

"I kicked you?" I attempted to look blank. "Kicked you? Ha, ha, ha." Nobody joined in my laughter. I looked at Micky who was sorting out comics. I looked at Alka who was admiring herself in the mirror above Micky's bed. I turned my gaze toward Anju, and saw her looking at me, so I pretended to scrutinize my shoes. The sound of receding footsteps prompted me to look up again. Anju was gone.

"Job done?" I asked Micky.

"Yes. Success achieved. Package passed," he replied telegraphically.

"What the hell are you two jabbering about?" Alka demanded. "It's rude to use code in public."

"Oh, nothing," Micky replied. "Let's get on with the math problems."

My heart beat wildly. "Nothing at all," I chimed.

Suddenly there was the sound of metal against concrete, followed by a gush of wind, followed by a bang, and a loud voice.

"Here are your comics," Anju yelled, banging my priceless possessions on the table, the comics that I had preserved so well; I took care to bind each one separately and stamp my name on each to make sure she knew they came from me.

"Trying to act smart with me, eh?" She caught Micky by the collar. "Look, you bloody toad, you know very well I don't read love stories. Don't you? Then how dare you do this?"

I did not utter a single word while this hurricane discharged its fury. The tone of her voice scared the wits out of me. After all, I was a follower of Mahatma Gandhi; therefore non-violent – and did not wish to speak, hear or see evil. She looked at me for a moment. I shifted my gaze to the math problem. I expected Micky to shift the blame on me, but amazingly, he did not. He freed himself from her clutches by pressing her wrists hard. I heard her scream.

"Yeah, yeah," retaliated Micky. "You don't read love stories. You're still a little baby who does not want to pervert her mind with such comics. Yeah? Ummmm…" His lips protruded out as he said, "Kiddo, go read your nursery rhymes. Baa, baa, black sheep, have you any …"

"Will you shut up?" she shouted. "Who the hell do you think you are, a bloody scholar of …"

"Why don't you just get lost? You know, poof, vanish? You're getting nothing. You don't know how to handle them properly, the nerve, throwing them down like that in front of the person who shares them with us! It's preposterous, outrageous. It's disgusting, it's …" On and on he went, at times using totally irrelevant words.

Anju, too, left no stone unturned and retaliated furiously until she was completely exhausted. Micky, of course, never tired of quarrelling.

Seeing him getting tough and so rude with Anju angered me, but I took no action until I recalled that a few minutes back she had saved me from Micky's onslaught of ridicule. Now, she had mishandled my comics, *my comics*, not Micky's. I looked at her, losing out to him, and something in her brown eyes made me screw up my courage to the point of some decision. I decided to go to her rescue.

"Look, Micky," I said, trying to sound commanding. "Is that the way to talk to a girl?" I looked him straight in the eye. "After all, what has she done? She threw my comics down on the table, that's all. *My* comics," I stressed, "not yours."

"Oh, dear. Oh, dear." Micky was furious. "You're ready to forgive her. If I had done that to your comics or books, you would have shouted your head off. But Anju is Anju, your idol, your whatever ... she can do no wrong."

"Micky," roared Anju, "if you utter one more word, I'll push you down the stairs."

"Just try it. I'll screw you dammit."

They glared at each other.

"You get out of here. Vanish. Now." Micky caught hold of Anju's arm and attempted to throw her out of the room.

"Leave me alone!" she screamed.

"Please," I persisted. "Please stop. Please."

"Tell her that."

I continued my persistence. " That really is enough. It's time to stop."

"Oh, well," relented Micky, "if you say so. Otherwise, I would have clobbered her."

Anju's face turned a dark shade of red – definitely not a blush. "What? You gonna bash me?" She clenched her fists.

"Look, please, please stop Micky," I begged.

Alka, who had been quietly admiring herself in the wall mirror above Micky's bed, seemingly unaware of the tussle, joined in.

"What's happening to you, Anju and Micky? Your behaviour's deteriorating. I shall have to talk to Papa about this," she said firmly.

"I'm sorry for creating such a scene, Vicky," Anju apologized.

I was not quite sure why she apologized in my presence. I was confused. Was she also trying to impress me like I was trying to impress her?

"Oh, that's okay," I said modestly. "You needn't apologize, but I would suggest that you guard your temper."

I was astonished – no, astounded – at my own self! I had spoken a whole sentence to her. Imagine! And that too, without stammering! Did it mean that I had overcome my shyness? I hoped so.

"I'll be leaving now, since you have no more math problems," Alka said, getting ready to leave, soon after Anju had left. "S'long, Micky and Victor." She walked to the door.

"S'long," responded Micky.

I did not realize we had decreased by one until Micky pinched me. "Goddamn you, can't you wave good-bye to a girl when she waves to you? There is something called courtesy, you know."

"Wha ... what ..." I exclaimed in astonishment. Where was I? Where was Anju? Was I not just playing badminton with her? Was I not losing every time, despite being a good player, just to hear her melodious laughter over and over again?

"Why are you staring at me so blankly? Hello! Anybody home," Micky said sarcastically and knocked on my head. He was clearly irritated. "You're always trying to teach me manners. How about yourself, man?" The taunting continued.

"I ... I ... was thinking of something else."

"Anju?"

I did not reply.

"You're really a gone case Vicky, you bloody daydreaming idiot."

"Yes, it was a sort of dream, but I'll make it a fact, you just wait and see."

"I'm waiting, I'm waiting," he chimed, closing his books.

6

Micky sat opposite me on my bed. He had come over with the comics I gave him the day before. He was so un-understanding! Now that he had come over to my place, he was obviously going to take replacements, and that meant a no-no to my going to his place, which meant no Anju.

As soon as I laid my hands on the comics, I flipped through the pages of the love stories, expecting to discover that love song – my confession – was untouched. *It was not there.* I looked at Micky who sat calmly with his arms folded across his chest, smiling.

"What type of humour is this?" I asked, nonplussed. "The song I put in here ..." I showed him the comic book.

"It's with her," he chimed musically. "Ding dong. It's with her."

"It's with her," I grumbled absent-mindedly as I flipped through the comics again. "W ... What?" I suddenly realised what he had said. "It's with her? Oh, please. Please. I mean how did it happen? No, you must have taken it out."

"Honestly, I did not. It is with her."

My heart beat rapidly. "H ... How?" I stuttered. "She ... She had said that she did not want these comics." I was curious and anxious, simultaneously.

"Well, soon after you left, I carried out an experiment. Thought it might help." He paused thoughtfully as he picked up my pillow, and started looking hard at it.

"You've always been so helpful," I praised him. " Could you, I mean, would you mind continuing ...?"

"I tucked the comics under my shirt, and into my pants, and acting mysterious and alert, as if being watched, I went to Anju, who was at the time sitting in the balcony on the first floor." He paused again.

"Then?" I pressed my hands together into the bed, my curiosity unbounded.

"Then what? I looked over my shoulder, pretending that you were still around and I was doing something that you would not have approved of." Yet another uncalled for pause.

"Please continue."

"Slowly and with great deliberation, I pulled out the love stories from under my shirt, they were hidden away in my trousers, you know, and lightly dropped them in her lap."

He made the whole thing sound very mysterious. I glanced at him questioningly.

"She looked up, startled, and I put a finger to my lips. 'Shhh.' I whispered that I had managed to persuade you into leaving the comics behind and I had brought them to her.

I added, 'He doesn't know, ' and she accepted them."

"When she returned them this morning," I continued from where he had stopped, "the song was missing. I suppose?"

"Yes." He smiled. "So?"

"So?"

"She loves you, yeah, yeah, yeah. She loves you, yeah, yeah, yeah," he sang the Beatles song.

"Shut up."

"The next batch of comics?"

"Choose them yourself. Four Harvey, four love stories."

"I want THE PIRATE, by Harold Robbins."

"Four Harvey, four love stories."

Micky buttoned his shirt as I talked to his mom. She held a glass of milk in her hands as she waited for Micky to finish dressing.

"You know, Vicky, I wish you would teach my stupid son some manners just for his own good." She paused. "It's for the good of your friend that I am saying this. Lately I've received several complaints about his behaviour."

"Oh, forget it, Mom," intervened Micky as he bent down to tie his shoelaces. "It was Anju's fault, not mine, and you know that."

"Well, Auntie, I am not that mindful of my manners, or etiquette, either," I said modestly.

"Don't be modest," she said smiling. "Why are Anju and Alka saying that you are the most decent, well-mannered and etiquette-conscious boy they have ever met?"

I was flattered. So Anju had been talking about me? I must admit that to impress her, I had patiently gone through Emily Post's book on etiquette. I did not regret the effort.

"Well, it depends on you," she said with an exaggerated sigh.

I looked at Micky who was fastening his belt. "I'll try, providing he cooperates."

"May we come in?" asked a voice from the doorway.

We turned at the sound, and there stood Anju and Svati, smiling. And, my nervousness returned. This was just not right! Just a couple of days I had talked to her, and now I was back to my old frustrations. What the hell was wrong with me?

"Come in, come in. Hello, Anju and Svati," greeted Micky's mother.

Before we could say anything more, Svati turned to Micky, fluttered her eyelashes, and asked for his biology book, which he handed over after a few minutes of searching.

"What do you need that book for?" asked Micky's mom, handing Micky the glass of milk. "You're still a couple of years his junior."

"For some reference work," answered Svati flipping through the pages. "You know our teacher, don't you, Auntie?"

"Mr. Tangri?"

"Yes. He gives extra credit if our work is above standard. So if an intelligent girl like me cannot get extra credit, then who shall?"

Micky finished gulping down his glass of milk and turned to me and said, "You're unusually quiet today, Vicky."

I stammered, "Ar ... aren't I as usual?" I began perspiring.

He scratched his empty head and repeated my last two words. The girls giggled and his mom smiled. I think she knew what was going on. Damn them all. Svati returned Micky's book with the excuse that it was too tough. Micky smiled, and his mom had an I-told-you-so expression.

As soon as the girls turned to leave, Micky called Anju's attention to the book I had brought for her, *The Mystery of the Pantomime Cat*, by Enid Blyton. She picked it up and thanked me, before rejoining her friend. I wiped my forehead with my handkerchief, which became so wet that it could be wrung dry, and put it back in my pocket.

"Want a glass of water, Vicky?" Micky's mom asked and left the room. I looked at Micky and a smile lit his face.

"Move, damn you," I shouted at him, to lessen my anger.

On our way downstairs I heard two voices. "Which one is it? Lemme see." "Be patient." I increased my pace.

As we walked in the park that evening, I made up my mind to say *Hi!* to her at the next encounter. I know it was an extreme, too much for me, but there had to be a first time. I could not avoid it forever.

If I do, then how will I ever get Anju, I thought. This gave my resolution a stronger foundation. *They made fun of me today, I thought, but I'll show them. Yes, I will.*

Frankly, I was scared. I remembered my resolution, at the same time hoping that I would not encounter her. I mean, you might wonder what could be so frightening about saying hi to a girl. Nothing really. I had shaken hands with Alka, and there had been nothing frightening about that. But, Anju was different; I mean, I felt differently about her. And that was what created all the difference.

I said some last minute prayers and took the plunge, and started ascending the stairs to Micky's floor. It required all the courage I could muster.

As I reached the first landing, I saw her sitting in the balcony in a cane chair with the Enid Blyton book in her hands. Dressed in a blue silk frock, she looked beautiful. I opened my mouth, and shut it immediately.

Her mother was sitting next to her chopping vegetables. I averted my eyes and ascended further, then halted after taking a couple of steps when my ears perceived a familiar voice.

"Vicky?" It was Micky's mom.

I turned and saw her sitting next to Anju's mother.

"Yes, Auntie. How are you?"

"I'm fine," she replied and crooked her finger at me, calling me closer.

I complied. Anju's mother looked at me as I attempted a smile. I noticed Anju was pretending to read, and my ears grew red.

"Don't go upstairs yet," Micky's mom requested.

I raised an eyebrow.

"I have arranged a math tutor for Micky, and he is upstairs now."

"Well, then, I'll be moving on. Could you please tell him to come over later today if he can?"

"He won't be long now," she said, looking at her watch. "Ten minutes more. You can wait that long, can't you?"

"I suppose."

"Vicky," she looked directly in my eyes, "would you mind answering a question for me?"

"Not at all," I replied, and plastered a smile on my face. I did not dare look at Anju.

"Why do you go for a walk in the evenings?"

What a stupid question, I thought. "We get bored sitting at home all day, doing nothing," I paused, did some quick thinking, and added, "or studying, so for recreation, we walk."

"Do you ever indulge in eve-teasing?"

My composure immediately vanished. So Anju had complained. "Eve-teasing, Auntie?" I looked at her forcing a blank and uncomprehending look in my eyes.

"Yes."

I glanced at Anju, who was still reading. It was a cover-up, for I noticed a coy smile.

Complaining about me? Disgusting.

"Where'd you get that crazy idea? Do you think I'd get involved in such activities? If you don't want me to come over anymore, just say so and you'll never see me again. But, this kind of accusation, Auntie?"

She was taken aback. "I'm not talking about you. I'm talking about Micky."

"I cannot answer for Micky," I replied, in a suitably defensive, but hurt tone.

"Oh, dear. You've been standing all this time," she exclaimed. "Anju, please get Vicky a chair."

"That's all right," I said hastily. "I'm leaving, anyway."

Anju deliberately got up and went inside, ostensibly for a chair, but she stood just inside the screen door, giggling.

"Send him over to my place, Auntie. Day after tomorrow I'll be leaving for Kashmir and will be gone for a couple of weeks, so ...” I deliberately left the sentence hanging.

“I would have called him,” she said apologetically, “but you know how everyone at school is grumbling about his grades.”

“Good-bye, Auntie,” I cut her off, and turned to leave. I am not sure what made me do it, but I turned back and said to Anju’s mother, “Good-bye to you, too, Auntie.”

Micky kept some comics on the bed and sat down beside them. We were in my room.

“Yes?” he said, looking at his watch.

I told him about his mother’s conversation with me. When I finished, he burst out laughing. “That’s too much.”

“What the hell?” I was bewildered.

“You know what? You’ve been ridiculed again? You have been made fun of again.”

I begged him to be more explicit.

“I have no tutor.”

“I don’t understand.”

“That eve-teasing business,” he continued. “Anju complained all right, and I joined in to describe the situation, and how you ran away.” Another laugh punctuated his explanation. “It ended up humorously.”

“Why did your mom ...?” I was still unsure just what was going on.

“All my mom was doing was teasing you.”

"How did she know about me?" I had a hunch, but just wanted to confirm it.

"Yesterday when Svati and Anju ...'

"I understand."

He suggested a walk, but I declined, so he left.

I put my sketch pen down and yawned. I was making a chemistry chart – part of a holiday assignment – and since I was at home and not intending to go out till it was completed, I did not feel it necessary to dress up. I had on a pair of old trousers, a cotton vest, with various colour marks on it where I had wiped my hands and ruler, and no shirt. I yawned again and climbed down from the dining table atop which I had been sitting with my chart.

A knock on the door interrupted me; it was Micky. As I let him in and tried to close the door, he stopped me.

"Put on your shirt, quick," he commanded.

"What?"

"She's coming upstairs."

I hurriedly put it on and heard a knock at the door.

"I'll open it," Micky said, moving towards the door.

"No." I caught hold of him. "I will."

He stepped back, and I opened the door slowly. I was looking down. When I raised my eyes I saw a pair of boy's shoes partly covered with denim jeans. *Boy's shoes*? I looked up and swore; it was Micky's cousin.

"Damn you."

The bastards laughed.

"Okay, okay, that's enough. Get out."

"So soon?" Micky looked at his cousin and then proceeded to admire my work on the drawing sheet. After a moment, he said, "Vicky, I need your bike."

"What for?"

"We're going swimming."

"What time will you return it?"

"Four p.m."

He took the key, came closer, took my chin in his hand, shook it and said, "Ummm ....ummm. AK. AK."

"Get lost!" I yelled.

7

Nothing exciting or significant happened during the next three weeks. Not because I avoided Anju – I relished her company – but the simple fact was that I had gone to Kashmir with my parents. Kashmir, the heaven on earth, the Switzerland of Asia, was anything but pleasant for me. The place was great, no doubt, but since I was away from Delhi, I could not visit Anju; I was finicky the whole trip.

Had she been with me, we could have enjoyed a lot of things together. We could have enrolled for a skiing course at Gulmarg, and skied mornings, returned for lunch, then gone again, for something else.

While we were in Sonmarg, my mom and dad re-lived their honeymoon snowballing each other. I watched them and thought of Anju.

At Daksum, three of us went for long walks. It was tranquil and beautiful, but again, no Anju.

In Srinagar, we often left our houseboat at night and went for Shikara rides. It could have been as beautiful for me as it was for my parents, but I did not have Anju, my special one, to share it with.

It was one full moon night as I sat in the Shikara, with my legs stretched out, gliding smoothly over the waters of the Dal Lake, looking up at the sky admiring the night. I could hear the swish of the oars in the water and see the galaxy in the sky with its Milky Way, and the glimmering stars stretched across it, the moon calmly resting in the centre. My imagination ran wild. The stars looked like a necklace of pearls adorning the moon. I missed her so much, it hurt. The beauty vanished and was replaced by pessimism. Kokernag was another lousy park.

On the return train journey, I watched out the dirty carriage window as everything unrolled, monotonous, and at times, sinister. The combination of hills, rocks, bushes, ruins, and occasionally dusty farmers in their fields now seemed uninteresting. Even the book I had with me remained tucked under my pillow ... I had not even bothered to open it. I know, it was very unlike me.

We returned to Delhi the day before school re-opened, and I was unable to make my usual visit to Micky's place; I had to shop for back-to-school supplies and get things organized for the following day.

A few more hours won't matter, I consoled myself. *I'll see her tomorrow anyway.*

8

Bubbling with anticipation and anxiety, and dressed in blue trousers, white shirt, a striped maroon tie and belt, white socks and highly polished black shoes – my school uniform – I reached school at eight twenty in the morning. We had ten minutes before school started to greet friends and classmates.

Class teacher's period was right after assembly. It was a free period, nicknamed "zero period".

Being good friends, Micky and I always sat together and raised hell in class during roll call.

"Enjoy your trip?" Micky asked.

"No, I kept thinking of her." I told him about the trip and the journey, and all the places we had visited. "But I could not appreciate it. I have ... Present, Ma'am ... I have some photographs of the panoramas and a thirty minute movie. You can see them sometime. Er ... how is she?"

"Fine, of course."

"Did she ... did she ...?"

"No, she did not ask about you."

Had this fool been practising mind reading, I wondered.

"You're sure?" He nodded and I continued, "I mean ... well, forget it, I'll know in a few ..."

"Now may I please say something?" Micky asked.

"You have my permission, sir."

"There is something new." He had my full attention now. "Anju has acquired a taste for books – no more comics."

"So you want me to start lending her books?"

"Well, yes, but I have a great idea. Instead of asking her choice and then you buying the book to lend her, I suggest you make out a list of books you have on hand. That way she can choose what she wants to read from what you already have, and you'll save money."

"You're talking sensibly for a change."

He tightened his fist to hit me.

"You can have the list this evening, or let's say tomorrow in school. Okay?"

The bell rang, and the class teacher's period ended. I did not get a chance to talk to him about her that day except during lunch break. We ate our lunch at a spot where I could see Anju, but she could not see me. Eating was quite a difficult chore in such circumstances, so Micky considerately devoured half my lunch, and the quarter that was left over came home with me and joined the contents of our waste bin.

I could not go to his place that evening since I was supposed to make a list and catalogue my books, and as I possessed a sundry collection – nine hundred and three, to be precise, most of the evening was spent classifying and listing them. I had never bothered to do that before, nor had I visited a friend so frequently in the past. I had not lent a book or comic for over a couple of years. This may have aroused suspicions at home, and with my neighbourhood companions.

"How come you're classifying and listing your books today?" Mom could not resist asking when she brought a glass of water I requested.

"Oh, I thought I should know how many books I have, and their authors."

It was a lame excuse, but all I could think of at the time.

"Don't you already know?" She eyed me suspiciously.

"The list will come in handy when I exchange or someone borrows my books," I replied, praying to God she would leave me alone.

"I see that you have again started lending your books. Don't you remember your earlier experiences?" She reminded me of the books I had lost, because many people simply forgot to return them, or had lost them.

"That's why I am cataloguing them." I tried to sound convincing. "This way I have a running inventory."

"I suggest you don't lend them out again. You know how upset you get when someone does not handle your books your way," she insisted.

"Suggestions, suggestions." I exploded. "If you must know, this is for a girl I'm trying to get acquainted with." I looked away, expecting a scolding.

Instead, she said, "Why didn't you say so? You thought I wouldn't approve, right?"

I nodded.

"Well, son, I have no objections. Besides, I already know about it."

I was bewildered and asked for an explanation. She smiled affectionately. "You may have failed to notice that last night at ten thirty, when the programme, Sunday Requests, was on, the song "Serenade of Love", was played on the radio, from Wing Commander Victor Sood to Miss ..."

I cut in, "I know. Were you listening, too?"

"Yes. Even I like music, you know. Here, I'll help you with the listing," she offered.

I did not know what she was thinking, but I could well imagine the subject – I was growing up.

"I can do it. It will take all evening. You needn't bother, but thanks anyway."

"As you wish." She gave up. "Oh, the rice must be burning." She scurried to the kitchen, and I thanked God as I resumed my tedious task.

I pushed the pin into the chart with my thumb. We were making an exhibition at school of the outstanding work done by students during the holidays – projects they had done on their own using various media and sources of external information on themes outlined in their curriculum. I was busy assisting the teachers set up the exhibition. The place where we used to play table tennis during milk and lunch breaks was laid out with albums, models and charts. A few of my charts and albums were there, showing I was a prize winner. I was exhilarated by the chance to impress her. Micky was also an assistant, and working alongside me.

"It took me all evening to prepare this," I said as I handed over the list of books to him.

"It'll pay off, man," he replied, accepting it and tucking it in his sock. "I'll give it to her this evening."

We pretended to be busy as a staff member headed our way. After he left, we resumed the broken link in our conversation.

"Yesterday I told her that you were back," Micky informed me in a tone that made the blood rush to my cheeks. Luckily, he was not looking. "At first she hesitated talking about you." He paused to put a pin in his mouth. "But presently, she asked me a hundred and one questions. It was like a volcano erupting."

"What sort of questions?" I asked, picking up the roll of tape that had slipped through my fingers.

"The way you ask questions about her," he replied casually, bending down to pick up another chart.

"Oh." I said no more knowing he expected me to plead. I also knew that if I did not pursue the subject, he would finally speak on his own, which he did.

"I told her you were a misogynist, you know that girl hater thing, when she first wanted to be friendly with you."

I remained expressionless, having had enough experience with his sense of humour. He did not appreciate my lack of response.

"Aren't you furious with me?" he asked.

"No," I replied casually. "In fact, I'm glad. I have given up the idea of pursuing her."

"What?" He was astonished and stared at me with open mouth.

We continued talking and working.

"You've got to come over today," he said as we went for a drink of water. "I'll introduce you again, and you can ..."

"I'll see if I can manage it," I replied.

We quenched our thirst and went back to conversation, and work.

I did not go to his house that evening; I was not her slave. I was the master of my will. The idea of reverse psychology, which Micky had told me about, seemed to be working. If my absence was conspicuous, good; she would grow fonder of me. It was a pleasant sensation to think that would be waiting for me. I decided to test the old proverb – absence makes the heart grow fonder ...

I was thrilled to discover that I had willpower. I managed to win the tug of war with my mind and coerced myself into staying home the whole evening. The feeling of triumph did not last long, though, and soon I felt like a dunce. To my disgust, I discovered I could not concentrate on anything – books, comics, food, or drink. Even my favourite Cliff Richard songs did not help. All I did was brood over Anju, so I gave myself up completely when Cliff Richard began to croon "Theme For a Dream'.

She paced Micky's room with a worried expression, lifting a magazine, aimlessly flipping through it and throwing it on the bed.

"Why hasn't he turned up?" she asked Micky, looking impatiently at her watch.

"Oh, he'll be along. What's eating you?" Micky replied and laid down on the bed.

"Go call him," she said through quivering lips.

"Aw, forget it. He doesn't have a phone anyway. He'll turn up."

"Please, please, Micky," she pleaded. "For my sake, please go to him. Call him over. I've never asked you to do anything for me before. Please."

"Then don't ask me now."

She began to cry, and Micky gave in.

It was late evening and four of Cliff's LPs had slipped by my record changer unknown to me, when suddenly I heard a familiar knock at the door that roused me. The door opened and Micky entered.

"Hello," I greeted.

"No one home?" Micky bolted the door behind him.

"No. Well?"

"You stupid fool, did I not tell you to come over today?"

"You told me." I stressed 'told'. "So I did not come. I am not her slave. Anyway, if you had cared to invite me, I ..."

"As if you aren't ever ready to jump at her command," he sneered. "How do I usually invite you? Keep your bloody mouth shut," he said, gesturing with his hands. "It's up to you whether you visit me or not. You come to my place just to see her, anyway."

I remained quiet.

"Anyway, let me tell you what I came to tell you. At seven o'clock she came upstairs and stayed a half hour pretending to read 'Stardust', and when you did not turn up, she left. I gave her the list."

"Tell me about it," I said, my heart thumping against my chest.

"About what?" He stared at me blankly.

"I mean, from the beginning, when you gave her the list, and the conversation that followed."

"Oh, that? I had tea with her. After tea, when she came upstairs, she questioned me about you. Maybe, she's become a helluva lot interested in you, pal."

"Yes?" I responded as if I had no grey matter.

"I said maybe, see?" He resumed the link. "I handed her the list, saying it was for some other girl. She immediately blew up, cursed you, thought better of it, and asked me if I was joking. I said no, so she returned the list and left in a huff."

"Haven't you missed something?" I asked him patiently. "Didn't she say something about her ... I mean, she must have said something about me."

"Yes, she did, as I've already told you. She cursed you. Ah, yes," he recalled, "she said she did not expect you to be that kind of guy. What kind, I don't know. By the way, she's jealous of the other girl."

"Good," I said, rubbing my hands together.

He smiled.

"Where will this bluffing lead to, Micky?" I suddenly realised that I was rubbing my hands together without reason.

"I was just joking. I told her so, later. You see, I was trying to detect her feelings for you, that's all."

"Shut up," I said with false imperiousness. "What type of books does she read?"

"Same old Enid Blyton."

"Take one of them to her."

9

I bit into the apple at 4:37 p.m. I had just returned from school and was having an evening snack. I took out my school diary and quickly flipped through it till I reached the page with today's date – Math, exercises twenty and twenty-one for Monday; English, not important; Russian, finished in class; no homework due for submission the next day.

I rested a while before bathing and dressing, after which I fixed my hair in a jazzy style and dabbed some of my mother's French perfume on my collar. As I viewed the guy in the mirror, I had to admire him.

I look more handsome than Adam, I thought, and blushed. The image blushed back, causing me to blush a little more and so forth till I turned my back to the mirror.

It was like a habit now – the bike ride, ringing the bell, admiring the evening, listening to the bicycle wheels, and watching the sun set as I pedalled my way to Micky's.

As I clicked shut the lock on the bike, something else clicked open in my mind – my resolution. The gaiety vanished, and a pensive mood replaced it, as I realized it would require all my guts to say a *Hi!* to Anju, and I was not even confident that I could muster them all together at will.

But, it's high time I tried, I said to myself. Otherwise, this trying game could go on forever, if I did not learn to control my emotions. *I'll prove to her that I'm a smart guy.* Determined, I put my foot firmly on the first step.

Heaving a sigh of relief, when I did not see her on my way to the second floor, I quickly reached Micky's quarters. It did not take long for him to dress.

"Let's go."

We descended the stairs and stepped out the gate, when I heard, "Hi, Micky."

We turned to find Svati and Anju waving at us from behind a big tree near the gate.

"Hi, girls," returned Micky.

I was afraid to utter a word for fear of making a fool of myself, and I did not wish to ruin the evening.

"Victor," Svati said, as if she were attacking me. Anju smiled. I tried to remain expressionless, since Anju was listening. "I hear you own around seven hundred books."

"Yes," I replied, hoping I sounded cool.

"Do you have any by James Hadley Chase?"

"Quite a few." I was so cool, I could detect that Svati was getting irritated. "Fifty-seven to be exact."

"Which ones?"

"I don't recall their titles." I pointed at Anju. "She's ..."

"He has so many books, he can't possibly remember all the titles." Micky came to my rescue.

"She's got the list," I continued, pointing towards Anju, who smiled again; her smile drove me nuts. I wanted to stay right there, tell everybody to shut up, and peacefully watch her smile.

"May I borrow some of them?" Svati broke into my thoughts.

I glanced at her. "Sure. Which ones do you want?"

"Any ... any will do." It was her turn to stumble.

"Okay," I replied. "I'll bring a couple of them tomorrow evening. All I ask is that you take good care of them."

Anju smiled at me and patted her hair, while Svati glared. Maybe Anju was rejoicing at my victory with conversation.

"Let's get going." Micky pulled my sleeve.

"'Bye Anju and Svati," Micky shouted over his shoulder as we turned to leave.

"'Bye, 'bye Victor," came the response, and I tripped over my shoelaces.

As we strolled in the park, Micky kept praising me, punctuating it by pointing out the pretty young girls walking past. He told me the conversation had been pre-planned, but I simply ruined the fun.

I kept my half-full bottle of Limca in the crate outside the shop where we had stopped to quench our thirst. I didn't know why, but I could not drink any more, and that was quite unlike me. I had a presentiment of disaster. What it portended, I could only guess. I made an effort to dismiss it, ignore it, but it just refused to go away. It was just too strong.

"What's wrong?" Micky asked as we left the confectionery shop, the same one where I had bought Cokes for Anju and Svati a few days earlier.

"Let's go back to your place," I said. "I'll pick up my bike and push off. I don't feel like shamming around today."

As we approached Micky's place, the feeling grew stronger.

Something's going to happen, I thought. And something did happen, which may prove that I possess ESP. I had no option but to go to Micky's place, as my bike was there, and I did not wish to walk back home.

As I wheeled my bicycle out on the road, the presentiment suddenly grew stronger, so strong that I could sense danger right behind my back, and that's where it was.

"Victor," called Anju, popping out of nowhere with that horrid friend of hers, "here's your book." She handed me the Enid Blyton book. "Thanks a lot."

Before I could respond, she added, "May I have more?"

What a serene voice, I thought, *such calm, as if she were chatting with an old friend.*

Suddenly several things happened at once. I got cold feet – cold everything – yet I began to perspire profusely. My legs swayed, and since I was leaning on my bike, it tottered. I lost my voice, my tongue turned dry, and I could not speak. My mind became paralyzed, and I was unable to check the rocking motion of my bike. Finally, it grew so violent, the bike fell over, and since I was resting on it, I fell on top. It must have looked like a jumbled up lump – from a distance – my position and the bike.

The girls giggled, Micky whistled, and I stuttered, "I ... I ... wi ... will get y ... you some more if you ..."

Before I could complete my sentence, the girls disappeared into the house, leaving me with Micky.

As soon as I gained my feet, I fled from the disastrous spot, leaving a taunting Micky behind.

I reached home dripping wet. As I analyzed myself in the mirror – shabby hair, torn shirt, and four scratches on my right palm – I was dismayed. Fortunately, no one was at home or I would have had a hell of a time explaining.

Nuts, I thought, *I was a real dunce, a born fiasco. Frightened of a girl, and I called myself a boy? Damn!*

10

It was the only inducement, in fact, the feeling that I experienced whenever I thought of Anju -- plainly passion.

A person in a normal frame of mind, devoid of passion, that is, would not have dared to venture even close to Micky's place after the embarrassing episode of the other day. Not for a few days at least, particularly when the possibility of an encounter with Anju and Svati still loomed large, but I did, and that too, the very next day.

There was a difference, though. I was determined to talk to her this time, no matter what happened. At worst, I would be laughed at, again. But, I was quite used to that by now. On the other hand, if I succeeded in talking to her, I was sure that I would conquer her – no girl could oppose those three little words, if she liked the speaker, at all. I was slowly learning the ways of the world, courtesy of Micky.

As the clock at Anju's place struck seven, I jumped off my bike. Surprisingly, she was nowhere to be seen. I locked my bike, and still no Anju appeared. As I climbed up the stairs, I encountered Micky coming down. After we exchanged greetings, he said, "You go on upstairs, I'll be right back." I continued my ascent.

He came a few minutes later and informed that he had gone to take a phone call from his mother, who said she would be late, and so Micky would have to stay at home for she was expecting guests.

"No stroll today," Micky informed me apologetically. I got up to leave after saying that I understood, but he caught hold of my arm and made me sit down again. I did not resist because that was exactly what I wanted.

"We can't go for a stroll, but we can do other things."

"Like what?" I asked making myself comfortable on his bed.

"Like finding out with numerology whether she likes you or not," he said, his eyes twinkling.

"But I don't remember the 'fundas' that well," I replied.

"No problem. Yesterday I was searching for my chemistry notes. I did not find them, of course, but I found something else – a book on numerology. I recall that you had once mentioned your interest in the subject, so I just kept the book aside for you. I'll go get it."

There was something else about Micky – he had a marked propensity toward ostentation. Though uninterested in heavy reading, he collected books on occultism, philosophy, psychology, and such subjects. He wanted people to see his collection and admire it, besides praising him for reading at such an intellectual level. Also, as he had once confided in me, he could pick up such books at real throwaway prices from the pavement markets. This habit of his, nevertheless, proved an advantage for me as I was deeply interested in occult, and could always delve into his treasures.

“Here.” He threw the book on the floor, sending clouds of dust in the air. He picked up the book, inspected, and then threw it down again.

“Can’t you handle your books a little better?” I asked, picking up the book and cleaning it with my handkerchief. “Have you ever seen any of my books in this condition? Now you understand why I don’t like to lend them to you?”

“Does Anju handle your books properly?” he countered.

“We’ll leave her out of this,” I said, opening the book. “Why do you throw your books around to dust them? Damn it, they should be dusted properly with a rag. When will you learn to respect books?”

“Forget the lecture.” He glared at me. “How do you find things with this?”

“Well, if you want to find out the nature of a person, you write down his name, then add up the numbers corresponding to the alphabets in his name – the list of corresponding numbers is somewhere in the book. If the sum is a two or three-digit number, then you add the numbers signified by the digits again, till you arrive at a single number. You should also add up the birth date numbers ..." I explained the basics to him in great detail, which took almost an hour. When I finished, I recalled that I had brought a book for Svati, so I unbuttoned my shirt and pulled out the book.

"This is for Svati," I said, placing the book on the bed.

"Anju's sister is getting married soon, and her fiancé is here tonight. Anju, Alka, Svati, and the others are busy with the couple, you know, having fun at their expense," he explained Anju's absence. "I was with them a while ago. Poor chap, I pity him."

"No chance of seeing her today?" I asked with a raised eyebrow.

"Why not? It's been over two hours since they began. She'll get tired of it soon," he forecasted.

As we were beginning the calculations in numerology, Micky told me about his latest love.

"The girl next door, has absolutely flipped over me, I swear."

I encouraged him to be more explicit. He ventured into the smallest of details about her actions and reactions whenever he was around, and then added, "I even saw her naked."

I tried to change the subject at this juncture. "It's almost eight. I'd better be going."

"Shut up," he replied and continued telling me how he had managed to 'see' this girl. "She knew I was watching from the kitchen window, but she still did not put her clothes on." He got excited. "She even turned in my direction and started moving her hands up from her ankles to her thighs and on to her ..."

"How can you be so sure that she's in love with you?" I made one more attempt to divert his train of thought.

"You want to know?"

"Yes." I had to listen patiently as he pursued the subject. I was waiting for Anju to leave the family gathering and come upstairs so that I could have my daily dose of her smile.

"Watch," he said, going out on the balcony. He made some funny noises with his mouth and to my astonishment, the girl next door came out into her balcony. I could not see her face clearly, for it was getting dark.

Micky waved to her, and she reciprocated. They started their own private chat in sign language, while I rested my forearms on the railing, riveting my eyes on the balcony below.

When Micky finished, I told him that Anju was free. He came over to where I was standing and looked down. Anju was sitting on the railing, while Svati stood beside her. Micky waved to them, then took my arm and started for the door.

"Wait," I said going back to his room to pick up the book for Svati, and the book on numerology. Had I known what those waving gestures meant, I would never have moved out of Micky's room. But I did not know, and that was that. It was unfortunate, but the truth.

Halfway downstairs, Micky began to whistle a tune, which was unusual for him. My mind rushed to the ultimate conclusion that Micky may have arranged another 'attack'. I was growing wiser, and I prepared myself. By the time I reached the first floor, I was determined that neither cockroaches nor caterpillars, neither hail nor storm, neither Anju nor Svati, could lead me to create another scene. I silently prayed to God for help.

Micky and team exchanged greetings. Then I was '*hello-ed*' and in turn, I acknowledged everyone.

"He's got a book for you," Micky informed Svati. "A Chase."

"Finally," she said, sighing. "I thought he'd forgotten." She took the book from me, flipped through the pages thoughtfully, pausing briefly here and there, and said, "Oh, I think I've read this one."

"Fine," I said. "I'll bring another one tomorrow."

She handed the book back to me. "Can you get me *No Orchids For Miss Blandish*?"

"Okay." I looked at my watch. "I'd better go."

At this point, Micky gave the password. "Vicky," he called out.

I turned to face him.

"Would you like to have two Tintin comics?"

Now, this sounded too generous, coming from Micky. Something was fishy.

"Wouldn't mind," I replied cautiously. And, suddenly a feeling portending danger began building, and the attack started.

"Hey, Victor, you in his class?" Svati asked, and for the first time I noticed her. She was around fifteen, fair, with long black hair wound into a thick pigtail dangling down her back. She was about the same height as Anju. She could be in Anju's class, but I was not too sure of that. She was in our school, for I had seen a number of times in the corridors, canteen, etc. Wearing jeans and a pink skivvy, she looked fairly attractive.

"Yes. Why?"

"Just because." She hunched her shoulders. I looked at my watch, and Micky must have winked at her or something. "You must be as old as he?" She continued bugging.

"Not exactly. I'm a year and a half younger," I replied.

"You know, Anju," Micky butted in, "he's been waiting for you since seven o'clock."

"Whaddaya mean?" I stormed.

Anju gave me one of her haunting smiles.

"Okay, okay, cool down." Micky patted my shoulder.

"I was wondering," Svati persisted, "how come a boy of your age is interested in Tintin? On the one hand you read Harold Robbins and on the other Tintin."

"What she means is," Anju intervened in that musical voice of hers that always drove me crazy, "isn't it a bit childish? I mean, aren't you too old to be reading Tintins?"

So that was it. I was prepared this time.

"By the way," I asked Micky, "who's lending me the Tintins? I prefer not to read them to answering all these questions."

"They're just ragging you," Micky confided, in a stage whisper.

"Oh." I turned to the girls. "Before I answer your questions, may I ask one?"

"Sure," Svati replied.

"Of course," chimed in Anju.

"Miss Anju," I forced a grin, knowing my ears were turning a deep shade of red – but I did not care; I had combed my hair over them so it would not show. "How old are you?"

"That's crudely put," she said, baffled. "You never ask a girl her age."

"Why?" broke in Micky.

"Well, all right," I said, ignoring Micky. "I know you are fourteen, and I think reading the Enid Blyton mystery series is rather childish. Don't you think so, Miss Kapoor?"

"Well ..." she said, knowing she was trapped. She glared at Micky and then turned to me. "You did not answer my question, so I won't answer yours."

"But I will," I exclaimed. "I ..."

"Don't bother." She raised her hands, palms out, as if in self defence. "I insist that you do not answer."

"Well, since you are so insistent, I won't bother," I said, bubbling at having conquered the scene.

"How considerate!"

I attacked Micky next. "Now that I have passed the test, may I please have the Tintins?"

"Test? What test?" He looked as if caught off-guard. "Anju," he called out, "Tintins."

At this moment someone else entered the scene. At first impression I judged him to be a man of considerable potential. He was on the better side of handsome, age around nineteen. He was tall and wearing a light coloured pair of trousers with a checked shirt safely tucked in to accentuate his expensive belt. His presence was imposing, not demanding. He was well-built and robust, with a Van Dyke beard, moustache, side-burns – attractive to the girls. Normally, I do not scan people so minutely, but this guy dominated the scene as soon as he appeared.

"Hi, Anil," greeted Micky, when he caught sight of him. "When did you get here?"

"This evening," he replied in a low pitched voice that reminded me of a bass drum. "Enjoy your break?"

" Anil, this is Victor, my class fellow."

We shook hands.

"Victor, you say? The girl-hater?"

Everyone began laughing.

"Have a good break?" Anil asked, turning to the gang and ignoring me.

"Well, sort of." They continued talking, with Anju and Svati joining in, finally settling down to planning a movie for the next day. None of it included me. Feeling rejected, I decided to leave.

"Excuse me," I intervened. "I ..."

"Look, Anju, everybody," Micky said imperiously, "you have silenced this poor chap."

"That's okay. I was just leaving."

"Gotta see someone?" Svati asked, grinning. "At this hour?"

"No, I've got some school assignments to complete."

"Okay, 'bye," Micky said. "Oh, yes, those Tintins. Anju, get those two Tintin comics, the ones I gave you yesterday."

As Anju departed to get the comics, the others resumed their conversation, still ignoring me.

I took the comics from Anju, and descended the stairs.

"'Bye, Vicky," Anju said.

I nearly slipped on the stairs, regaining my balance in the nick of time.

"Good-bye," I replied.

"See me tomorrow, okay?" Anju invited.

That kind of talk made me nervous.

"Yes, and thanks for the invitation," I managed to mumble, and slipped down the last step.

As I unlocked the bike, Svati called, "Hey, Victor, may I have that Chase novel you brought? I'd like to read it again."

"Sure. Come get it."

"Bring it to me."

"Sorry. If you want it, come and take it."

I wheeled my bike out the gate, and looked up at her. "Want it?"

"Wait," she said, as Anju shoved her. That gesture made realise that maybe I had finally won Anju.

It marked the beginning of our friendship, a friendship I hoped would last a lifetime.

Part Two

11

I closed my eyes. I had just returned from school, and though not really tired, I was comfortably sprawled on my bed. I was bored and nursing a feeling of resentment for Anil. Just imagine! Taking Anju to a movie on the first day of our developing relationship! I mean, it was the first time that she personally invited me over. Well, I supposed I could do nothing about it.

I thought over the happenings of the day once again. I had encountered Anju several times in school, whether by coincidence or deliberately, I was not sure. Perhaps it was just plain *kismet.* The first encounter was early in the morning session, near the water-cooler. She smiled at me, but I did not respond. Several of my classmates were around, and I was afraid my feelings would show; my friends and classmates were under the impression I hated girls. The past seven years of school life, I had never even voluntarily talked to a girl, let alone smile at one. I usually opted to change my seat if a girl sat next to me. I even ignored compliments if they came from a girl. Of course, this did prompt many to deliberately perform actions that made me uncomfortable. They often teased me, like deliberately sitting next to me after making sure that there was no vacant seat left in class for me to shift to, or they would sandwich me, or pin me against the wall and tickle me. When they got through, I was usually on the verge of tears. If they ever guessed I liked Anju ... I shuddered just thinking about it. I wanted to be close to Anju and look at her, but I could not face having my friends find out about us.

It was Saturday. School was out at one in the afternoon, and I was sitting on Bus Number One. Bus Number Two, Anju's bus, was parked in front of us so that the rear window faced us. As usual, I was in the front seat beside the driver; Anju was on the back seat in her bus. I could see her clearly.

My bus broke down before it even left the school grounds, and most of us were transferred to Bus Number Two.

I boarded the bus from the rear door, and as seating was fully occupied, I found myself standing face to face with Anju. This time, I made no effort to move away. I had a funny kind of pleasant, tingly sensation which felt good. I remained silent during the ride home, but it was a comfortable silence, as if we were communicating secretly.

When I reached home, and thought about getting ready to go to her place, I recalled their movie plans, so I stretched out on the bed instead, and let Anju pervade my thoughts.

12

The door opened, and Micky found me lying on the bed, reading. It was Sunday and still morning, the clock showed a quarter to eleven. I looked shabby as I had not yet gotten out of bed or had a shower.

"Well?" I asked, yawning.

"I'm going to poison your whole day," he grandly announced.

"Yeah?"

"She no wanna talk to you."

That got my attention. I sat up. Where had I gone wrong? I spent days trying to make her acquaintance, and when I almost succeeded, something had to go wrong. Murphy's Law. Who can fight it?

"She says you break your promises," confided Micky, and after a pause, with mock innocence, added, "Do you?"

"Promises? What did I promise?"

"I don't know ... something about visiting her last evening, maybe?"

"Weren't you all planning to go to a movie with whatsizname ... Anil? Why would I go to your place, knowing that?" I was almost screaming in frustration.

"She did not go, dammit." He also raised his voice. "She said she had a date with you."

"D … d … d … date? With me?" I was devastated. "But I never promised anything."

"You said you'd be coming, and when you say something you should mean it, shouldn't you?" After a pause, he added, "Anyway, I did not say anything. She did all the talking."

"Look, Micky," I pleaded, "you gotta help me." I caught hold of his sleeve. "Can you … I mean, would you please explain the blunder to her and apologize for me?"

"Now, why on earth should I do that?" he retorted. "You blundered, you apologize. I won't."

I knew he just wanted me to grovel, plead, fall at his feet, and feed his ego, whatever.

"I … I … I'll get nervous again," I tried to explain. "Please, won't you do it as a favour to a friend?"

"No."

"Please. Look, I'll loan you *The Godfather*."

"No. Look, Vicky …"

"You can have *Dracula*, too."

His voice began to waver. The temptation was too great.

"Permanently," I hastily added, without thinking.

He gave in. It was an offer he couldn't refuse.

"Oh, very well. I'll explain it to her. Come over today before the Sunday movie on TV. It might prove profitable."

"Okay." I hoped she would believe him.

"May I have a fifty percent advance?" he demanded.

"Which one?" I suddenly realized that I was at his mercy now. I could have kicked myself for getting in such a bind. I knew he would ask for *Dracula*, the one I offered permanently. If he took *The Godfather*, to be returned later, I might forget my promise. The shot had left the gun, and I needed him, so I could not go back on my word.

Anyway, I thought, *Anju's forgiveness is worth more than the petty price I am paying.*

"*Dracula*."

"Take it," I said reluctantly.

It was an hour before the TV movie – sufficient time, I thought. There was little activity on the way to Micky's; the streets were deserted. As the soft plumes of dust whispered secrets to the whirring cycle wheels, the hot wind hammered doubts into my brain. What if Anju refused to listen? She could be stubborn.

Micky was asleep when I reached his house. I half expected it, for no one would have liked to exert oneself in the oppressive heat of that afternoon.

"Whenever you turn up," Micky's mom greeted me, "I always imagine I smell something fishy."

"Fishy?" *She's mocking me again*, I thought to myself. "That's ridiculous, Auntie," I said, acting surprised.

"How come?"

"I'm a vegetarian. I don't eat fish."

"Very clever," she replied with a grin and ushered me into Micky's room. "Wake him up, if you can. He's been sleeping soundly for over four hours." She closed the door behind her.

I tried for several minutes to rouse him, but in vain. To add to my annoyance, and desperation, Anju turned up. As soon as I heard her, I bolted the door from inside. I wanted to hear the story firsthand from Micky. I slapped him hard on the cheek, with no effect. He had that stupid smile on his face. I pulled his hair. Nothing. He was probably enjoying a good dream. I looked around the room, and my gaze came to rest on a glass of water on the bedside table. I grinned. When I finished, he jumped up, thinking it was raining.

"Really, Vicky!" he snapped. "I'm surprised at you."

"No, sir," I said. "You are not surprised. I am surprised. You are astonished."

"Okay, okay, cut the crap." He yawned. "What brings you here to disturb me? I was having such fun with that girl next door ..."

It is not my nature to bear malice. I wanted no row, so I maintained my cool and came directly to the point.

"You invited me over," I reminded him.

"I did? Well." He took out a comb from his hip pocket and started using it.

"She's outside and will be coming in any moment. Quick, tell me what she said. I want to understand the situation before I face her."

"Said? What ...?" He yawned deliberately.

"Did you explain to her?"

"Explain what?"

"Look, Micky, enough is enough. Cut the funny talk. Also, please understand, I am desperate."

"Oh, yesterday's misunderstanding?"

I nodded.

"Well, sort of, I mean, she said okay, but don't talk to her about it. You know, no point in scratching old wounds or whatever..."

I heaved a sigh of relief. "You had me scared for a while. I really didn't imagine she would so understand, but I guess love does that, eh?"

He was not listening; he had gone back to his dreamland.

A loud knock at the door brought him back into waking consciousness, and to his feet.

"Why did you bolt the door?" Anju demanded, as he let her in.

She entered in her unique style. "Were you doing something funny in bed? Hi, Vicky." I could see her exuberance drop a notch.

"Hi!"

"I did not bolt it," replied Micky.

I bit my lip. The creep was going to tell on me again.

"Since Vicky had no reason to bolt it, and there is no one else in sight, I suppose the door bolted itself," she mocked.

Uninterested in the banter, I looked at Anju. She wore a skirt and sandals instead of the usual slippers. Her half covered feet, with no nail polish, were as beautiful and fair as her face.

"Maybe a grumml did it?" she persisted.

"A whatl?" asked Micky.

"Not a whatl, a grumml," she corrected. "A grumml is too small to be seen by the naked eye. It's responsible for wrong things that happen. Follow me?"

I don't know whether he followed or not. I did. So a grumml must have somehow penetrated my skull the day before and made me believe that Anju would not wait for me. I was innocent, I decided ... and beamed.

"Like," questioned Micky, "how do you know all this?"

"I just read it in a comic book, and like, for example, bolting your door, or loosening your shirt button, or upsetting a dog's dish, or rolling up the carpet, or blowing important papers away, or making a pen leak, or ..."

It was a golden chance to save my *Dracula* and *The Godfather,* so I jumped to grab it. If I managed to explain everything to Anju myself ...

"Or like making me think that you had gone for a movie yesterday, when you actually hadn't, right?"

I glanced at Anju and took a step forward. She took a step backward. I must have looked a sight; I had not bothered to dress up as usual because of the confusion. Instead of looking like Adam, I thought, I was looking more like his janitor. As far as I knew, love did not depend on clothes or money or appearance, anyway. I didn't think she was criticizing my appearance; she just looked surprised.

"Uh ... oh, I almost forgot that you were here." She was not furious, but soft. "Why are you so shy around me?"

"Um, well, I'm not ... not now."

"Anju, you have my permission to leave," announced Micky, glaring at both of us.

"Keep your gab shut," Anju snarled.

"Anju ..."

"I have already told her; don't pursue it," intervened Micky.

It was a question of my two favourite books. "No, you haven't," I snapped.

"Yes?" Anju said. "Vicky, may I ...?"

"Wait, let me talk first. I came to beg your forgiveness for what happened yesterday."

"What happened yesterday?" She sounded genuinely surprised.

I looked towards Micky, and he picked up a magazine. Something was not right here!

"I did not turn up yesterday while you missed your movie waiting for me." I looked at my shirt's third button as I spoke. "I hope you will not let that ruin our friendship." I looked up as I finished, and noted that she was looking at her feet. I was puzzled.

"I'm the one who's guilty," she said as Micky scratched his head in embarrassment.

He excused himself and left the room.

"I did go to a movie yesterday. Honestly, I did not want to, but Micky and Anil forced me." Her foot scratched the floor. "I was hoping you would forgive me. Actually, Micky told me that you had come over last evening as I had invited you, and then returned home disappointed. In fact, I asked Micky to sort of talk to you on my behalf and explain the blunder. He refused at first, but when I offered him three chocolates, he agreed."

"Good grief!" I exclaimed. "You know what Micky told me?"

I told her everything, adding a bit here and there to make my words stronger. "I gave him *Dracula* as fifty percent advance payment." I clenched my fists. "I'll kill him."

"No, I will."

"You may, after I have finished."

"No, ladies first."

"I'll tell you what, let's do it together."

"Micky!" we both shouted together at the top of our lungs.

He came in, realizing he was in bad trouble.

"Chocolates," demanded Anju, and Micky fished them out from under his pillow.

"Vicky," Anju turned to me, "would you excuse me? There's a TV movie starting in a few minutes, and I want to watch it."

"Okay. 'Bye." I smiled at her.

"'Bye."

I noticed the dimples in her cheeks and the twinkle in her eyes.

"My *Dracula*?" I started towards Micky, and he took it out from the bedside shelf. "Really, Micky, you're something else."

He shrugged.

"Good-bye, Mr. Mukesh Mehra," I snapped, and banged the door behind me.

13

My hands tightened on the brakes as I pulled to a stop. I had gone to Anju's place as per my usual practice. I say Anju's place, for I saw no reason to climb all the way up to Micky's floor; I did not wish to speak with him after what he had done the day before. Besides, it was my first evening with her, and I wanted it to myself.

She was standing outside the gate, in black trousers and a frilled pink jumper, talking to Svati and a couple of other girls.

She took leave of them and walked over to me. I suggested a walk in the park, and she agreed. Walking with her was a pleasure, a feeling too wonderful to try to explain. My cup was full and my head in the stars. I wanted to touch her, hold her hand, and caress it. We did not talk much, for I could think of nothing to talk about except love, and I hardly thought it to be appropriate at the time.

For the first time since we met, she seemed shy. I am not sure whether it was my imagination or a fact. Micky said that even the most uninhibited girls feel shy around the person they love – in the beginning, at least – and Micky certainly was an experienced man.

"Are you feeling shy? Because of me?" I asked, feeling braver than usual.

"Me? Shy of you?" She laughed out loud, but not in derision.

"Why are you not talking today? I mean, why are you so quiet?"

"What would you like me to talk about?" She sounded self-conscious – something new for her.

"Nothing in particular. It's nice, just being with you," I said, smiling.

After a while, we decided to turn back home. We stopped and had Cokes. I've had hundreds of Cokes in my lifetime, but that day, it tasted superb; in fact the whole evening seemed out of this world. I had never before realised how nice a walk through the park could be. The place was not exactly deserted, but still I experienced the bliss of solitude with her. The grass was the same, but sitting on it with her was more relaxing and pleasurable than sitting on foam cushions. The flowers were the same, but today I sensed their beauty in a new way. Their fragrance around us was in a new dimension when compared to her smile. I watched her as she busied herself plucking blades of grass. She was really beautiful. She looked at me with tender warmth in her eyes.

After we had walked back to her home, and said our 'byes, a feeling of loneliness overtook me. The spell of the evening seemed to fade and was replaced with gloom.

Oh well, I consoled myself, *it will only be a few hours before I see her again, and those hours will be spent dreaming about her.*

I was filled with anticipation as I closed my books and started on my 'sacred rites of pride' – getting ready to leave for Anju's place. I had finished my studies for the day, knowing from past experience that I would not be able to concentrate after my visit with her.

I parked my bike at the usual spot near the entrance to the stairway at her place and looked around hoping to spot her. Seeing no one, I proceeded to Micky's floor. I could have asked for her at the ground floor, but whoever answered the door might have questioned my identity and the purpose of my calling, and I was not too confident that I could have answered to a reasonable level of satisfaction. I thought it better to forgive Micky and wait at his place.

As I reached the first floor, Svati appeared. There were three persons sitting on cane chairs on the balcony: Svati's chair faced the stairway.

She greeted me with, "There he is," and followed it with a "Hello!"

The others greeted me as I nodded and smiled. The evening was off to a nice start. To my astonishment, Micky begged forgiveness.

The gesture was quite unexpected. I figured that he was not really repenting; he must have been asked to say he was sorry.

I gave Anju the comics, Svati a smile, and Micky a nod. After five minutes of discussion, we decided on a game of carom as no one except me, Micky and Svati was in favour of a walk. I was conducted through the door behind Micky's chair, and along a short corridor, full appetising aromas coming from the kitchen, to Anju's room behind the hall.

It was small and gaily decorated. The walls were pink, and the doors and windows had matching flowery curtains. We sat on a square bed in the centre near the wall opposite the door. A chair and study table stood in one corner. It was a lovely arrangement.

As Anju laid out the carom-board, a girl of about twenty one intervened. She was rather tall, and wore an evening dress, a safari suit with a frilled shirt front. She asked for Anju's pen. Anju formally introduced me to her sister, Anita, the one planning to marry soon. She asked me a few questions in a thin, high-pitched voice, but I forget what she asked or how I answered. I only remember one thing, Anju's face.

Then the question of teaming up arose. We decided on a match between the boys and the girls. I was not much interested in the game, nor was Anju, for that matter; the match was mainly carried on between Svati and Micky, while Anju and I stole glances at each other, or took a few points occasionally, frequently losing lots as penalties for fouls. Svati beat Micky, and the girls shouted with glee. Micky scowled, and I remained expressionless.

This is really too much, I said to myself finally, and decided to pay more attention to the game. I continued to wonder whether Anju's rosy cheeks were as soft as her heart. Being a good player, I wiped the board clean in a few minutes, leaving the girls scowling. We played six games. We could have won every game quite effortlessly, but feeling the girls would not appreciate that, we let them win thrice, to make the overall score even.

We chatted for a while afterward, made fun of our teachers at school, particularly my physics teacher who was courting a lady teacher in Anju's class. Anju stepped out to get drinks.

"It's really tasty," I told her, sipping the mango squash she brought. "Just the right amount of sugar and concentrate, and of course, chilled just right."

"I did not prepare it," she replied.

"Oh? I was wondering why it wasn't as tasty as the one at my place." I swirled a sip in my mouth and winked at her.

We burst out laughing. She served something crunchy with it. I could not identify it, for I was not paying that much attention; Anju had my full attention.

14

During the next few days we met regularly. I explained my past experiences with the girls in my grade to Anju and made her promise she would not talk to me or acknowledge me at school.

We met daily after school. Both of us reduced our routine visits to relatives, which were usually scheduled for evenings or during days off from school. We had our studies and home assignments to attend to, and too many other things to do, like seeing each other – we had no spare time! I continued seeing her daily at either Micky's or her home.

Our evening activities were not always planned. What we did depended on her mood. It could be anything – a walk, a play, a discussion, a game, or nothing at all. I never tried to touch her. I was curious to know how it felt touching a girl you love – when your hands touch hers, when your lips touch hers, when you caress her ... For the time being, I was content just sharing her company. Maybe she would not resist, but that just did not seem important to find out at this stage of our growing friendship.

15

I looked around and found a vacant seat next to the window. Lunch break had just ended, and the rest of the class was still pouring into the physics lab for a theory class.

The lab happened to overlook the playground, mainly the basketball courts, and since the teacher had not yet arrived, I watched out the window and noticed Anju in her gym outfit getting ready for a game of basketball. I was sure she had not seen me.

Presently the physics teacher arrived and began discussing Rumkorff's Induction Coil, explaining how the coil of wire, known as the primary coil, through which current passes, produces a magnetic field, which in turn ... He droned on, explaining the construction and workings of the coil.

I could not concentrate on the subject; I was too busy watching Anju. I wished he would excuse us like he had done a few days earlier when he was not feeling well. I guess my inattentiveness was quite obvious, because soon I noticed him glaring at me. Then he began to scold me, making me feel like an idiot.

"Really, Sood, I'm surprised. You're one of our best students and of all people ..."

He continued scolding, followed by a long lecture about the approaching secondary examinations. Before he finished, my head automatically turned to glance out the window again, and he dismissed me from class. That was too much. We had two consecutive periods of physics, and standing outside the class for that long was quite unbearable, not to mention humiliating; however, I stood without complaint.

As I stood out there, just outside the door, I did some thinking and finally concluded that probably Anju was distracting me from my studies. I was letting thoughts of her dominate my life to the detriment of my schooling. My grades had dropped a bit compared to the past. That was not a good thing, for sure. I resolved to do something about it. Perhaps, I should avoid her for a while. After all, it was a question of my career, something very important in life. Of course, relationships were equally important, because what was life ...

The bell rang indicating the end of the first period, and I suddenly realised that Anju would have to pass me on her way to her class. If she saw me standing in the hall, ousted from class, I would not be able to bear the humiliation. During the five minute break between periods, I begged pardon of my teacher, and with his permission, resumed my seat.

16

I had not been to Anju's for three days, when she just whispered sweetly in my ear, "This evening?" and completely destroyed my resolution.

During milk break, Micky and I were returning from the cafeteria, after eating a snack, when we passed Anju and her friends going in the opposite direction, which made it inevitable for us to come face to face, albeit for a fraction of a minute. As we crossed, I noticed one of her friends pat her on the shoulder and point towards me.

"Don't be silly," I heard her say, narrowing her eyes and pushing the hand off her shoulder.

The smile that was making its way to my face faded as she increased her pace, ignoring me completely. This, however, was our normal procedure while at school, though my emotions just failed to remain under control most of the time.

At lunchtime, since I had not brought my lunch from home, I took refuge in the cafeteria again, after sharing Micky's lunch. We drank water, since they were out of chilled soft drinks.

As I wiped my mouth with a handkerchief, Anju came by with a couple of her classmates, and I noticed that they were staring at me. Feeling self-conscious, I rubbed my forefinger over my upper lip as I waited for Micky, who was still drinking water.

"Move," he said, when he finished, and pulled me by the shoulder. I shrugged and followed him, but stopped after a few steps when I heard my name called.

It was Anju. "Victor Sood."

I looked at Micky who looked back at me questioningly. I shrugged, for I had no idea what she wanted.

"Yes?" I said, walking towards the girls.

"What is this I am hearing around school?" demanded Anju.

"What *are* you hearing?" I asked, puzzled.

"Rumours," she said acidly.

"Rumours?" I repeated.

"Rumours?" Micky was also puzzled.

"Yes," she replied.

"What sort?" I was really puzzled. Why was she acting like this? What rumours could have triggered that attitude? And of all the places, at school!

"You must have heard them, too," she insisted, her voice graduating to unfriendly.

"I swear I don't know what you're talking about."

"What's happened?" Micky asked.

"Tell us what you're talking about. I honestly have no idea," I said.

"The one about you knowing me too well," she said looking down.

I looked at Micky, and he seemed to be thinking hard. Anju surreptitiously closed one eye and nodded her head towards one of the girls.

I looked at Anju, faking a stern attitude. "Look here," I said, "you know very well that's crap. I don't even know your name. Since you know mine, may I ask who you are?"

"Shut up."

"Listen, you, whatever your name is. Watch your profanity. This is a school, and I'm not your friend. You have no right to accuse me. Don't you know how to talk to your senior? Why don't you just get lost?"

Micky stared at me, open-mouthed, not believing what he was hearing.

I softened and said, "Look, words won't hurt you, so stop worrying."

Anju turned to her friends, who seemed embarrassed. "You saw it for yourself," she snarled. "Let's move on."

As they did, Anju turned quickly and whispered, "This evening?" She turned back and said loudly, "Move, damn you."

My resolution vanished.

17

It was just the two of us – I and Anju, that evening and we were playing chess. Svati had not come as she was preparing for some class tests scheduled for the following day, and Micky had gone upstairs for a snack. The evening had passed in bubbling excitement compounded with high spirits. Then it happened. Right in the middle of our game, I remembered my resolution, and the joviality vanished. I tried to conceal my change of mood from Anju, but I was sure she sensed something was wrong, for the game became oppressive and we decided to discontinue it.

"What's wrong?" she asked, frowning.

"Nothing. Nothing at all, but I should be going, I ..."

"Something's wrong," she stressed. "You've been here only an hour."

"I ... I ... gotta go. Good-bye."

I bumped into Micky as I stepped out the door and made him drop the sandwich he was eating.

"Where're you going?" he queried. "Look what you have done."

"Home."

"So soon?"

"Something has happened and I have to discuss it with you. Can you come over to my place?"

He offered to walk me home.

"Something wrong?" he began as soon as we were out the gate.

"Yes, a lot," I replied. "I'll get directly to the point. Anju is distracting me from my studies, and it's beginning to tell. One day I was chucked out of physics class, and yesterday, Mrs. Gadi gave me a mouthful after class. Today, Mr. Dham called me to his chambers and gave me a long lecture. I've got to do something about it, Micky. This can't go on. You know our final board exams are approaching, and I can't afford to fail them by spending all my time thinking about Anju."

"So tell her to go to hell. Tell her she's a bitch and that you're going to cut it off with her. Tell her you don't want to see her face again. Tell her ..." he scowled, and his face turned all red.

"No, no, no," I said, stopping him. "I'm not saying it that way. What I mean is that I should reduce the frequency of my visits to your place. I think that's the best solution. What do you think?"

"I fully endorse it."

"You can explain it in a nice way to her and make some excuses for me."

"Whoa, whoa! Hang on! Why the hell should I?" he asked, while squinting his left eye and widening the right one.

"Please." I knew he would do it, after the usual pleading and coaxing. "You're my best friend; if you won't help me, nobody will."

"Well, okay. I'll try." He did not commit himself. "What will I tell her? What will you do evenings?"

"Me? I'll study."

"You can't study all evening, can you?"

I couldn't and I admitted it. "It's only when I'm near her that I lose interest in everything else. And the effect does not wear off that quickly, you know. We could do it this way: I'll come to your place, say twice a week or so and you don't bring her to mine. You can come over daily, of course. I know she won't talk to me at school. It's only when I am at your place that we ..."

"How's that going to help the situation?"

"I'll be able to concentrate on my studies. I have not submitted last week's math home assignment yet."

"So?"

"My studies are more important than females. Girls you can get anytime, but a career ..."

"Vicky," he said in a fatherly tone of voice, "it's not that easy to get away from a person you're so fond of. You may stay away from her physically, but your mind will play tricks on you. The farther you go physically, the closer you get mentally and emotionally. And considering whatever I know of you, you are not going to be able to get her out of your system, either which way. Even if you her cut her off, how is it going to affect me? No way at all, but what I suggest is that you think about it. There's still plenty of time before exams – about eight months."

"How about the end-of-term ones next month?"

"That's a month away, and she has her exams, too. She does not want to cut off with you. As for studies, don't people in love study? Do you think you are the only one who's ever been in love? Anyway, you shouldn't take this friendship so seriously." He paused, and then added, "It proves one thing: you're too young and immature for this sort of thing."

"Fifteen is not too young," I flared. "No age is too young to fall in love."

"Watching you, I can only say one thing : This is a crush which will soon wear off when you start taking an interest in other girls."

"This is not a crush, Micky. No girl will ever take Anju's place. I know that. How come I've never felt like this about any other girl?"

"Okay, okay, cool down. We've been talking for the past twenty minutes without any results."

"Because ... because I gotta study," I tried explaining once again.

"That's why I call it a crush. People in love don't behave like you; love is not necessarily a distraction, it's an inspiration." He paused. "Mr. Victor Sood, just shoo off. By the way, let me tell you that I'm not going to help in breaking this beautiful friendship. Both of you are my friends. People like you two need each other."

I walked the rest of the way alone.

I tucked my hands under my head and stared at the ceiling, as Micky's words echoed in my mind. *"People in love don't neglect their studies. Love is not a distraction, it's an inspiration."* According to him, Anju had been improving in her studies ever since she met me, for she did not want her parents to object to our friendship. She spent time with me, and also found time for her studies. Micky told me that she had formed a habit of studying early in the evening before I made an appearance at her or Micky's place. She knew if she did not perform well in the exams, our relationship would suffer.

Here I was, bungling everything, coming down from eighty percent in physics to forty percent, besides failing in math! A few days back, my class teacher had detained me for about an hour after school and tried to get out of me the reason for a sudden drop in my grades. Everybody at school was astonished at my poor performance in practically all subjects. I agree that I had never been an excellent student, but I had been consistently above average. Until now, that is.

No, I thought, *I've got to show them that I'm still good, if not better than before. I simply have to.*

I would continue seeing Anju, though sporadically. I finally decided to share my thoughts with her.

If she truly loves me, she'll stick by me, I figured. *If not, well ... I'll just have to be strong.*

At the back of my mind, however, I knew she would understand. I mean, she was too sweet, not to.

18

My thoughts and vision drifted to Anju. She looked happy as fifty of us stood on stage, while the results of our end-of-term exams were being announced. I did not stand first in the school, but I had the satisfaction of being in the top fifty, which was quite an achievement, considering that the school had more than four thousand students on the rolls. I had actually scored better in these exams than in the previous ones.

Anju had also fared well, with an aggregate of seventy-two percent, no mean achievement. She was first in her class. About a month and a half had passed since I had put an end to my poor grades; I was again respected by my teachers.

At first I had stayed away from Anju's place for several days, after explaining everything to her. She had been disappointed, but, understanding the situation, she accepted my decision. Micky began frequenting my place and brought me her messages. I discovered that I could concentrate on my studies again. After I caught up on schoolwork, I started visiting her again. Since I had opened up my mind to her, I felt more capable of handling our relationship with a little more maturity.

19

The sound of ringing bicycle bells brought me off the bed and out of my room.

It was the first day of our one-week autumn holidays which was traditional in our school; to provide the students a short break after each set of exams. We had decided to go camping.

The day before, Micky and I finalized a plan for camping out, and I suggested we take a few friends along.

"The more the merrier," I said.

"You mean Anju, don't you?" he asked, catching on quickly.

He's getting sensible, I thought.

"Well, yes. I mean, Anju, Svati, Anil, Ginny, you and me, and anyone else you want."

"Anil is not in town. How about taking Rahul along?"

"Sure."

Rahul was a classmate who lived a few doors away from him. "If you want that next door friend of yours, get her along, too," I said, teasing.

"You're a real pal, Vicky. Would you please ask her for me?"

"M ... me?"

"Please. Oh, please. Did I not help you with Anju?"

"I … I …? Good-bye," I blurted. "Tomorrow at six."

Six of us, two girls and four boys, set out on a camping trip as planned. We had been instructed by our parents not to spend the night out, and be home before dark. Since we lived in the centre of the city with no forests or woods around, we decided to bike to Ridge Road, which was an uninhabited place surrounded by huge trees, a sort of green wasteland, and camp there for the day.

Several roads ran through the stretch, but people seldom used them. We could always go further inwards where there were no roads and find a clearing for a camp, but then stories of mugging in the area had been heard, which made us a little wary. It was really a picnic that we had gone for, but I call it camping because we were spending the day in a deserted spot, in a place that resembled a forest sans wildlife.

We reached the spot at seven in the morning determined to spend the day no matter what happened. We were dressed in jeans and cotton tops. I had forewarned everybody that the paths inside the area had thorny bushes growing in abundance. As we entered the area through an opening in the natural hedge formed by the trees and brush, a spirit of adventure invaded us.

We cautiously proceeded further and soon heard a hissing sound. Thinking it was a snake, we pulled back, but it turned out to be my bike's rear tyre that had already found a thorn. It was no big problem, so we continued on our way, finally reaching our destination – a small clearing which I had never seen before, though I had visited the area often with my other camping friends. We manoeuvred our bikes through the winding paths, our minds full of the good time we were anticipating.

We had brought a hatchet and a tent with us, besides some cooking utensils and matches. We spread a cloth on the ground, and as the girls rested, we boys cut firewood and long poles for the tent. The work was exhausting, and we were compelled to rest every few minutes. Then, I got a bright idea.

"Hey, look," I called, "you carry on with the tent business, while I take pictures and a movie."

They accepted my suggestion, and I was excused from work. I set up the cinema camera, focused the still camera, and settled down on a rock. I announced that I was trying to get good shots to show at school; however, my intention was to photograph Anju and send the pictures to a photography contest, and of course, keep them for my personal viewing pleasure.

After the tent was erected, we discovered that six of us could not fit inside it. Cursing, the boys got up to re-shape it, and this time we all crowded in.

All this physical effort had made us quite hungry, so we pulled out the sandwich filling we had brought with us and decided to make some toast and tea to go with it. The girls worked hard to light a small fire, using bits of dry leaves, dry twigs and scads of matches, not to mention lots of patience. We boys offered to make toast on open fire, and ended up burning the bread. We offered to make tea and ended up spilling most of the milk in the fire. Finally, the girls got fed up and dismissed us, telling us to mind our own affairs, and leave the cooking business to them. We were only too glad to accept.

After we had eaten the sandwiches, we just sat around in the tent. I am naturally a fidgety person – restless. Being unable to lie down cramped up in the tent, and not really wanting to answer any questions about me and Anju, or listen to obscene jokes, I figured it might be a good idea to go outside and walk around a bit.

It was ten thirty in the morning, but the sun was brilliant and already perched high in the sky. There were no birds; they had gone somewhere to escape the heat. I took my camera along, just in case I found something interesting to shoot. I went around the tent to the designated cooking spot, and spotted

Anju. She, too, spotted me and decided to demonstrate her cooking dexterity.

"Boiling potatoes is a job for us girls," she said, with a triumphant expression. "You boys mess up everything. No wonder you are not allowed in the kitchens. Look, this is how you lift the lid of a saucepan."

"I'm looking."

She lifted the lid with her tiny handkerchief, and then dropped it on the toe of my boot, making a nasty mark on it.

"Oh, I'm sorry, Vicky," she apologized, looking up at me.

"It doesn't matter, but I have a feeling you're going to be sorrier when you see those potatoes."

"Oh, no!" she squealed as she stared at the saucepan.

Svati sauntered in, hearing the commotion. She was amused. The potatoes had disintegrated into a seared, black mess.

"Who told you to peel the potatoes before putting them on?" I asked.

"The potatoes I eat at home are peeled," she replied indignantly.

"Did you put any water in?" I questioned.

"Of course."

"How much?"

"This much." She indicated with the tip of her finger – about half an inch.

"Great," I exclaimed, and Svati burst out laughing. "Why did you not tell her how much water to put in?" I asked Svati.

"I wasn't around when she did it."

Our voices roused the others, and they came out and began criticising Anju and Svati. I stopped them.

"It could happen to anyone," I said.

Anju appreciated my gesture.

"Since it is early noon, I suggest we take out the ketchup, the leftover bread and fruits and whatever we have, and have an early lunch. Forget the cooking business. A little sustenance will cheer us up. C'mon."

We had a good lunch, and I decided to shoot some more film. We decided unanimously that I should take shots of someone kindling a fire by rubbing two twigs together. The gang gathered twigs and worked frantically, but failed to get a single spark. I wasted half a ten-minute reel of film in the bargain.

"No more shooting," I announced, disgusted.

We spent the afternoon munching chips, sharing anecdotes, and singing. I found Anju's joke the most amusing, though it embarrassed Ginny. The joke began with, "Once there was an intelligent Sikh ..."

At around three in the afternoon, we decided to have tea. We still had a little milk left.

"I'll make the tea," Micky volunteered, and we let him.

I surreptitiously winked at Anju, as I followed Micky out of the tent, ostensibly to take some photos of him. She understood. Svati saw the wink, and a naughty smile appeared briefly on her lips.

We sat on a rock behind the tent, shielded from the sun and probing eyes of our companions.

"Enjoying yourself?" I asked.

"Not too much ... but, well, it's different. It's better than being holed up at home."

"Suggest something to make it more interesting," I invited.

"How about collecting feathers?"

"That's interesting?"

"Very. Let's ... Please?"

"Okay." I gave up. Hurting her was not my line.

We looked around in vain for about fifteen minutes hoping for uncommon feathers, but there were none to be found. So, Anju decided to collect thorny plants instead, and I accompanied her. I could not let her do it alone, of course. Thorny fruits and plants were in abundance, and Anju hopped on happily. I took a couple of pictures to preserve the moments.

As we were returning to base, or tent, to be precise, Anju spied some oval shaped thorn fruit and decided to pick at least one. There was nothing to stop her except a narrow ditch between her and the fruity bush. Even though the ditch was not very wide or deep, it seemed unlikely to me that she would be able to cross it without assistance.

Good, I thought, *no more additions to the bag full of thorns I'm carrying.*

But, I had under-estimated Anju. She obstinately crossed the ditch in one jump, picked the fruit, and then tried to jump back. Now, she was not successful. As she stood at the edge of the ditch with nothing to hold onto except a thorny plant, and an uncertain expression on her face, I stretched out my hand to help her. She hesitantly took it and jumped.

I don't know what came over me, but I did not let go of her hand instantly, but continued to hold it. She made no effort to release it, either.

Just holding her hand gave me an indescribable thrill, a feeling I had never had before. A sense of affection, one I cannot describe, overwhelmed me as we stood there hand in hand, saying nothing. The world seemed to stand still.

With my eyes riveted to her face, I noticed something I had never seen before, something I never expected: Anju was blushing. She looked adorable and divine, head tilted to the right, eyes lowered, and the corners of her lips widening and contracting alternately. I affectionately pressed her hand. It was so soft, and she was mine, all mine, absolutely mine, nobody else's. Something clicked in my mind, and I put my other hand against her cheek.

"Fantastic shot," called out Micky, as he shut down my camera.

I immediately let go of her and demanded, " What are you doing here?"

"Photographing," he replied casually.

"You had no right to, damn you!" I was furious.

"Hey, what are you worried about? Isn't this your camera and your film?"

"Okay," I replied curtly. "Don't touch it again."

I was really upset at him for having broken the heavenly spell.

"I guess I can," he grinned mischievously. "Let's see you stop me."

As we approached the campsite, I begged Micky to keep the whole episode to himself. Everyone was packing up and getting ready to proceed home.

"You guys want some tea?" asked Svati. "We have a bit left over."

I declined.

I rode my punctured bike all the way home, not stopping to have it repaired. I was just so angry at Micky.

After we had seen Rahul and Ginny off, Anju and I lagged behind, as Micky and Svati pedalled ahead.

"I'm sorry," I said.

"What for?"

"For ... for ..."

"Forget it. I liked it."

We resumed pedalling, and I waved good-bye as she turned off at her place.

At home, my mother asked, "Enjoyed your outing?"

"Yes," was my short reply.

"Doesn't sound like it."

"This Micky has been giving me a bad time. I'll never go camping with him again ... ever!"

20

I pushed the pillow away and groped around. Where was I? Why was it dark? I felt my limbs for wounds or blood, but found none. The front portion of my shorts was sticky and smelled funny. I was confused. Then I realised that I was on my bed, and burst out laughing. Yes, it was a dream, a wild one ... the effects of touching Anju, I figured.

I am frenziedly pedalling my bike on my way to Anju's place, with Micky sitting on the frame in front, holding tightly onto the handlebar. He asks me whether I would be able to make it.

"Of course," I reply confidently. "It's only a short distance."

The scene shifted. I am working on a plaster model of Anju, and it is almost done. I am shaping her hand. It had to be completed that evening for her birthday.

The birthday party had begun, and most of the guests were drifting into the drawing room. Somebody put a Samba record on the big stereo system. Anju's place was gay with the sound of music and dancing, full of laughter, clinking of glasses and the chatter of voices. I suddenly remembered that I, too, had been invited. I tell Micky to wrap up my gift.

The party is on the ground floor, and I am on the top floor of the same house.

I reach the hall, have a good look at all the girls present, and stop to listen to their parents' conversation. They are praising somebody, and peering at Anju, admiring her new hairdo. I go over to Anju, kiss her hand, and she asks for her gift.

"I'll bring seven gifts," I answer proudly.

"Oh, how sweet," she croons and puts her hand against my cheek. "Get them quickly."

I run off to get them, and discover that Micky's room is a long way off. I meet Anil on the way, and we start walking together. I ask if he would be able to loan me some black sheets to cover Anju's statue. He replies in the negative, and we both get into a car that is passing by. Anil whispers something to the driver in front, and settles down comfortably. The car lunges forward. The road is quite wide, but the car can barely manoeuvre without touching the buildings on either side.

Micky is walking next to me in a long corridor. I tell him about Anil's behaviour, but he seemed to not care. I decide to ask him for his black curtains.

"What for?"

"To use as a backdrop for Anju's statue."

"Screw off."

The scene changes again. I am singing with Anju, "You and I Were Made For Each Other." I caress her hand. We are in a big park with lots of colourful flowers. Micky is sitting in a rose bush, plucking out thorns from his hand, and watching us.

I pull Anju close to me and run my fingers through her hair. She presses herself close to me and wraps her arms around my waist. I run my hands over her arms and finally reach her shoulders. I am about to press my lips to hers, when a hand taps my shoulder.

I turn around and am confronted by tough-looking guys in khaki police uniforms. They have menacing grins on their faces. One of them tries to take Anju's hand. She screams, and I apply a judo trick on the guy. He reels, falling backward, and goes through the windshield of a passing car. Another toughie steps forward and beckons me. As I get closer to him, he reaches out and punches me in the belly, but I tighten my stomach muscles and escape the pain. I get hold of his wrist, put my foot against his, my hips against the right side of his waist, and lift him up and forward; he reels away. I look at his companions and they run away.

"Well done," says Micky, patting me on the back. We go and sit in our car; Anju is already there. She puts her hand on mine and begins to fondle it.

We reach Connaught Place at eleven thirty in the night. I increase pressure on the brake pedal, and the car comes to a screeching halt. Men clad in dirty khaki uniforms, brandishing daggers and rifles, block our path. We have to pass through, somehow. But how? I turn towards Anju, but she is not in the car. I turn towards the rear seat; even Micky has vanished. I start thinking, and my palms begin to itch. I look out and I see one of the dirty men trying to rip Anju's clothes off. I rush towards him.

Somebody showers me with punches and tries to bang my head against the car. I dodge the punches and lunge my head into his stomach. He doubles up, as I run towards Anju, whose blouse sleeve is badly torn. I hit the man responsible on the jaw and injure him; I am sure his jaw is broken. As I bend down to check, I hear Anju screaming. I turn around to see a dagger aimed and racing towards my heart. I quickly manoeuvre out of the way, and the dagger goes straight into the heart of the man lying on the ground.

Another man lunges forward with a wicked grin on his face. I kick him on the chin, and he drops to the ground. I turn around and see that two of them have set fire to my car.

I turn to the right and see two more strong wrestlers moving in to attack, and realize that they are planning an ambush. Their hairy chests intimidate me, and a thought of running away brushes my mind, but I have to save Anju. And that is what matters, most. I have only one dagger with me, so as they approach, I cut a wide swath and open wide the stomachs of both of them.

The scene changes and there is blood all around us, and Anju is clinging tightly to me and sobbing. I pat her head as she wipes the blood from my forehead with her sleeve. I kiss her forehead, and then push her away. She looks astonished.

A tough looking character, in torn khakis is challenging me to a duel – a six-footer with a broad chest. I twist on my toe as he charges towards me, and kick him in the stomach. He lies writhing on the ground. A mini-man appears, and I throw my dagger at him; it enters his skull through an eye. He pulls it out and hurls it back at me.

Then the mini-man and the six-footer team up on me. I push the tall one away with a slash to his arm, but the mini-man gets in between my legs and trips me. Anju is terrified and keeps shouting for Micky, but Micky is not responding. I am lying flat on the road, as the six-footer picks up the mini-man and brings him down on me like an axe. I manage to roll over, and the man's head bursts open.

The scene shifts to Anju's place where guests are getting ready to depart. Anju holds my hand possessively and praises me. I am proud of having saved her. Suddenly I see a small boy with a deformed head sitting on the floor. He is saying something, but his words are not very articulate. I bend down to him and – it is Micky!

"I shouldn't have banged him so viciously, his brain has been affected, maybe crushed," I say. "Look, I'll show you."

I cut his head off with a dagger and slice a piece and show it to Anju's father. Anju keeps pulling at my hand. I turn to her and say, "Yes?"

"I'm bored," she complains. "Let's go watch a movie."

"I'm too tired."

She drops the idea of a movie, takes my hand and leads me to a sofa where I sit down with her in my lap.

The night is almost over, and I have to go home. Anju is sleeping with her head on my shoulder. I caress her cheek, and she opens her eyes.

"I've got to go," I say, pressing my lips to hers, going deep, searching, finding, reaching – a long kiss.

I pull myself away, and the dream ended.

21

The Censor Board had awarded it an "Adults only" certification. Fortunately, Svati's father had a friend who was the owner of Archana cinema. So, getting in would not be a problem; the problem was that the show was sold out, and the manager had only four tickets left from his special quota. We were five persons – Anil, Micky, Svati, Anju and me.

"I'm sorry," the man said, "but you can watch the evening show."

Anil had his car, so none of us objected. Everyone would have a way home after the show. It would be around nine in the night by the time the show ended, and not safe to travel in auto-rickshaws. The buses too were not at frequent intervals at that hour. We bought the tickets, then settled down to make plans for the rest of the afternoon.

"Let's go to Connaught Place," suggested Anju.

I seconded the motion. We drove down and decided to walk from Regal. There was a parking lot opposite, which was handy.

"Want to eat?" Anil asked.

"Not yet."

We strolled around Janpath and the Indianoil Building. Nearby was a shopping area, and there was a coffee shop that served fantastic cold coffee, so we decided to have a bottle. I liked the music better than the coffee, if you ask me.

At four thirty, we still had two hours to kill.

"I'm tired," complained Svati. "What's the fun in just loitering around in this heat?"

"I have an idea," I said. "Why not go to a record shop and ..."

"Yeah," interrupted Anju, "let's do that. It'll be fun."

We stepped into Rhythm Corner, a big store dealing in music equipment and music. The place had four sound cubicles, small rooms fitted with a stereo set and four chairs. We chose ten LPs and entered one of the cubicles, ostensibly to make a final decision.

"Oooo, beautiful," murmured Anju, smiling at me. "We can easily pass two hours here. Play Carl Douglas first."

The time flew quickly. The third LP was on the turntable, but I had little re-collection of the music. I had a better objective – watching Anju. She sat next to me, pressed tight against me – five of us had to accommodate ourselves on four chairs. I was getting this pleasant sensation, my body tingling all over, and I tried hard to keep it subdued because we were not alone.

"Sorry, but we're not buying today," I told the scowling shopkeeper as we emerged from the cubicle and made our way to the exit.

"Where to now?"

"How about some food?" suggested hungry Micky.

We went to De Ramble.

We had just come out of Archana after watching the movie "Friends" and were heading home. It was a beautiful movie about two teenagers who decide to live together as adults.

"Hey, you two," Micky said, "don't do that, okay? You'll suffer if you do." He gave us an I'm-telling-you-in-advance-don't-blame-me-later look.

Svati and Anil smiled. I blushed.

"Don't worry," said Anju to Micky. Then, to me, "Ignore him."

I wondered how she kept her cool.

I didn't take the wheel, the driver did. It was my cousin's Ambassador which I had managed to borrow after two hours of intense pleading and begging. He made it very clear that I would be the one paying for the fuel and the driver's food.

The sound of the horn brought Anju to the gate.

"You?"

"Yup," I said.

"Whose car is that?"

"My cousin's. Look don't waste time. I have the car only for a few hours. Call Svati, and I'll call Micky. Let's go to Budhha Jayanti Park."

"What for?"

"For an impromptu picnic. C'mon."

We spent around three hours playing cards, eating and talking. I repeatedly touched Anju's hand, just for the thrill of it. Call it childish, or whatever, but it seemed the natural thing. She did not object, and smiled often. I did not attempt to go any further, unlike the "Friends" story.

"Those two are a gone case," remarked Svati as she saw me deliberately throwing the cards Anju needed. She was sitting beside me, and by tilting a little to the left, I could see her cards. I couldn't bear to see her dejected, so I did whatever I could to make her win. I got my reward in her cry of joy.

I tapped her shoulder. She looked at me, and I gestured with my eyes: let's move out.

Micky must have seen it, for he said, "Yah, yah, get lost both of you. And, uh-oh, Vicky, since when have you acquired the courage to be so intimate with Anju in front of us?"

"Shut up, Micky," retorted Anju.

"You know what," Micky turned to Svati. "You know when we went camping ...?"

We fled, hand in hand, and sat down under a tree a short distance away from Svati and Micky.

"I'll soon be going away," I told Anju.

"Where?" she asked, startled.

"Don't be startled. You know I'm going to college somewhere after I pass Higher Secondary."

"Can't you get admission here in Delhi?"

"I don't know. It depends on how I fare in the HS exams and the entrance exams after that."

"What do you mean? My Vicky could never ..."

"Your Vicky?" I was beside myself with joy.

"You're going for engineering, aren't you?"

"Yes, but not here. My parents want to send me to England to study Bio-Chemical Engineering, a branch not yet available in India. They are checking out options for an educational loan."

"You could choose some other branch, couldn't you?" she asked.

"What would you like me to be?"

"A marine engineer," she replied, and blushed. "Why?"

She half expected my answer, for her blush deepened. "After all, it's you who has to cope with me the rest of my life."

"Fiddle," she said. "Me marrying a dunce like you? Never."

"Oh, well," I sighed putting my hand to my chest, "I'll try to find someone else. I've seen a lot of Hindi movies, too, you know."

"You dare," she said, clenching her fists, and we both burst out laughing.

"Don't forget to invite us," chorused Micky and Svati, suddenly appearing beside us.

"Wh ... where did you come from?" I exclaimed, cursing him for ruining the moment.

"We were sitting behind you," he informed me, "but you were so lost in each other you didn't hear us. I wish I had a friend like Anju." He mimicked actions from "Romeo and Juliet" which had been on TV the week before.

It was the last day of vacation, and we had gone to eat some spicy snacks, popularly known as *chaat* and *gol-gappas*. As it happened, Anju dropped one of the *gol-gappas*, or fried dough balls filled with spiced water, and it burst on the thigh portion of her trousers. Micky seized the opportunity and started to tease her. But when he became a little vulgar, she burst into tears, and rushed home. Micky, oblivious to the effect of his words, was laughing when I turned to face him.

"You'll never learn, Micky, never," I said, in disgust, and followed Anju.

"Hey, who's going to pay? I don't have any cash on me," Micky shouted after me.

The crying, laughing, quarrelling, making up, cursing, apologizing, talking, walking, sleeping, and dreaming continued. Life continued normally until December when I stopped going to Anju's so regularly. The reason was that Higher Secondary exams were due in three months and I needed to concentrate on my studies. I had problems with the numerical part of physics, and this time, since it was a question of my career, I simply had to do something about it. I could study all day, but after returning from Anju's place it was not possible to settle down for at least a couple of hours, and time was precious. I went to see her occasionally, particularly when I felt tired and depressed.

22

The occupants of the chairs in the front row were sobbing. I was in the third row. We were on stage and our school principal was at the mike praising us - our group of students, the outgoing eleventh grade. It was the last day of school. I wanted to release the gloom imprisoned in my heart, but crying was not appropriate for boys. I looked at my fellow schoolmates. Most of them would not miss me, or any of us on stage, for that matter, but I would. College life would be much different. In a way, it was the end of the disciplined era of my life.

I recalled the mischief we had gotten into these past few years. I had received plenty of scolding from my teachers, and I hated to be scolded, but I would miss my teachers who had imparted knowledge to us and laid the foundation of a secure future. I respected them.

It was our turn to say something. Our speakers broke down while reading the farewell speeches. It was genuine; each of us was under a sentimental spell. To show our respect for our teachers and our school, we offered them mementos, our tokens of love.

23

It was an evening in February and I was in the bathroom. Study leave had begun a couple of weeks before, and I was determined to make the most of it. I had spent the day locked up in my room, studying. A few minutes earlier, I had felt exhausted and decided to rest, but my mom talked me into taking a hot shower, saying it would relax me.

"Micky's here," my mom called out. I hurriedly dried myself and put on my clothes, as I did not want to keep him waiting.

I stepped into my bedroom, and a thrill rushed through me. It was a pleasant surprise dressed in violet trousers and a yellow, high-neck pullover topped with a violet muffler; Anju sat there flipping through my books. Micky was half sprawled on my bed. He had brought her over, for some comics, so he said.

"Oh hi, Anju. Hi, Micky."

"Hi, " responded Anju.

"You, here? A real surprise," I said to her.

"Just felt like seeing you," she replied.

"If you want," intervened Micky, "I'll sit in the drawing room."

"No need to do that," Anju said, giggling.

The door opened, and mother entered with a loaded tray in her hands.

"Micky," she said, placing the tray on the table. "Won't you introduce me to your lovely cousin?"

"I'm Anju." She introduced herself.

"Anju," repeated mother, and turned to me.

I nodded, and Anju blushed.

Mother began telling Anju what a dunce her son was, a good-for-nothing oaf and a few other embarrassing things.

"I know," Anju agreed.

"Look, mom, please," I protested.

"I wonder how you manage this idiot," she continued. "Micky, doesn't he fight with you? The way he quarrels with his sister is a caution. Why are you not eating anything?" she asked Anju as she offered her biscuits.

"Thanks, but I've already had tea," Anju told her.

"Oh, yes, you must have, but this friend of yours," pointing at me, "hasn't even had his lunch. No time, he says. And ..."

"Mom, please."

"Oh, well," she said shrugging her shoulders, and left the room.

"How do you like my place?" I asked Anju.

"I like your poster collection."

"Want some?"

"Wouldn't mind, but my parents wouldn't permit me to have them on the walls," she confessed.

"Good-bye, Vicky," Micky said, pulling Anju to her feet. She scowled.

"So soon?" I asked.

"Yes," she answered. "He made me promise only ten minutes. Anyway, now I can drop in anytime I feel like it, if it's okay with you."

"You're always welcome," I said.

"'Bye. Happy studying." That was my Anju. She went out, but stopped at the door, turned around and said, "Vicky, I like your mother ... even better than mine."

I was chewing on my pen the next time Anju came over. I didn't notice her at first, for I was lost in chemistry equations, complicated stuff.

She must have been there for a while. Finally, she blurted, "This is the limit, Vicky."

I turned around. "Oh, it's you. Hi!"

"What's the date today?" I could see she was smiling.

"What's the date today?" I looked at her blankly. "Why?"

"Just answer me."

"Well, let me think. It's the twenty-eighth. So?"

"So?"

"Oh my God!" I exclaimed. "Happy Birthday and many happy returns of the day."

"Thank you." She acknowledged my greeting with her hands on my shoulders. "This evening at five-thirty, okay?"

"I'm sorry, Anju, but it's only five days until exams. I can't possibly come tonight. I'm helpless. Please understand."

"Surely you can spare an hour or so," she said, disappointed.

"Not tonight. I'll make up for it later. Okay? Please."

She left in a huff. I wanted to run after her and make up, but the thought of my studies held me back. Not that it helped for the next couple of hours or so.

24

The hands on the clock kept moving, and before I realized it, exams had come and gone. I had done quite well, in my judgement.

I had not been able to contact Anju during the period between that fateful day and the end of my exams. But, now, that exams were done and over with, I resumed my visits to her place. She was still the same: lovable, beautiful, and charming. However, something seemed amiss; her fondness for me seemed diminished. It could have been a delusion, and I hoped it was, but I was not sure. My refusal to attend her birthday party had probably caused the problem. Micky mentioned that she had promised to introduce me to some of her friends that night and had been embarrassed when I did not show up. I felt miserable.

My efforts to make up were fruitless. I tried pleading, flattering, and apologizing. She was not hostile and she never avoided me, but I sensed that things were not the same.

One evening I folded my hands in front of her and requested she tell me what was wrong. That broke the barrier.

"How do you think I felt when you tried to shake me off during your exams?"

"But, Anju ..."

"Never leave me, Vicky, never," she cut in. "Promise me."

"I promise, my darling." I was hypnotized by the sincerity in her eyes. "I promise."

I took her hand in mine and slowly pulled her closer. It seemed as if I were floating on air. I could feel her arms tightening around my waist. My heartbeat grew faster and a strange sensation grew in the pit of my stomach. I pressed her closer to me, while I caressed her soft, silky hair.

"Promise, you'll never leave me, Anju, never," I whispered. "How would I live without you?" I fondled her cheek.

25

It was the last week of May, and exam results had been announced the day before. I had secured seventy-eight percent marks, and stood at sixteenth rank in the whole of India – next to the last name on the merit list. Anju was overjoyed. She knew, with those marks, I would have no difficulty with admission into a Delhi college. However, destiny had different plans for me. In fact, it had been ordained that I would not be staying in Delhi.

"You're avoiding me again on purpose, aren't you?" Anju shot me the stark question. "It's already been a week since I last saw you. I come over to your place more often than you come to my home."

"What? Why would I avoid the only girl I ever loved?"

"I don't know," she said icily. "But at the rate we are seeing each other, I'm inclined to think you've found other interests."

"Look, Anju, I ..."

"Yeah, of course, you're a brilliant guy," she taunted, "and plenty of girls in the neighbourhood are crazy about..."

"Anju," I cut in, exasperated, "this doubting is leading to trouble and having a negative effect on our friendship. You know I've been busy getting my certificates cyclostyled and typed and attested, besides filling up and sending my applications for admission to various colleges. I also had to confirm the information I got about the marine engineering course. It seems they're not taking any new entrants this year."

"I believe you," she said. "How could anyone disbelieve a lovable person like you?"

"Thank you." I pressed her hand.

"Why do you have to apply to all those colleges?" she asked. "You're sure to be admitted in Delhi College of Engineering with your marks."

"That's all right. Anyway, I have filled out the D.C.E. form also. My parents are planning to send me to England for Bio-Chemical Engineering, provided I get selected and they manage a loan."

"You promised me ..." she said tears springing to her eyes.

"Now, look, Anju, please ... I haven't received a call from anywhere as yet. I don't want to hurt you."

She quickly wiped her tears and handed me a card. It was an invitation for her sister's wedding.

"You'll simply have to come," she asserted, and added, "don't forget," as a precaution. We sat for a while after that discussing the future.

I was having a terrible time explaining my absence. Anju's sister had been married the day before and I was in trouble. I had been unable to attend the wedding even though Anju had repeatedly reminded me. It was the last day to submit forms for the D.C.E. and I spent the whole day at it, travelling in buses and standing in queues. When I returned home that evening, exhausted, I fell asleep, and my mother had not bothered to wake me up until it was time for dinner. By which time, it was too late to go for the wedding.

"Look, Anju," I tried to explain. "How could I help it if there was a long queue? I had to submit the form that day."

"You did it on purpose," she said. "You don't see me often, you don't attend my parties, you don't bother to meet my friends, and I know you are going away soon. Are you thinking of breaking up with me?" A tear coursed down her cheek – a weapon against which I had no defence. "You simply don't like me anymore."

"Where do you get all those crazy ideas? Please forgive me one more time," I implored. "I won't give you a chance to complain again, I promise."

She forgave me. "I love you, Vicky."

I was relieved and flattered.

Soon it was the middle of 1976, and I was busy with the competitive entrance examination for the I.I.T., Indian School of Mines, and Delhi School of Architecture. Anju was busy with her holiday homework, once again, but we still found time to meet each other. It was a year since we had first met. In a few weeks or so, I would probably leave to join college somewhere, and we wanted to make the most of the time I had left in Delhi.

I was now considering taking up mechanical engineering, and marine engineering the following year. However, if I failed to get through the tough competition for marine engineering the following year, I could always go for the one-year training program, after graduating from mechanical engineering. The problem was that the education system in Delhi had been re-vamped that year and now ten plus two had become the stepping stone for entrance into marine engineering college, instead of Higher Secondary, or the eleventh grade. So, I had to spend one year at some other college, in order to complete twelve years of cducation, and comply with the new standard.

Anju agreed with my plan of going for mechanical engineering for now.

Time moved on, and the results for I.I.T. were declared. I did not make it.

"You failed," she guessed, optimistically.

I admitted that I had not made it to the qualifying list.

"Great," she said. "Now you have no choice but to join the D.C.E."

You could not argue with Anju; she always had things her way. I was selected for admission in Delhi College of Engineering, and shifted to its hostel soon after.

I sneaked out the side door of the hostel building where I had been living the past few weeks, and slowly made my way to the iron fence surrounding the campus. Every time I spied a face in one of the windows, I crouched on my knees and hid in the tall grass surrounding the building. It had not been cut for a long time. As I climbed over the fence and was trying to jump off the other side, I heard someone call, "Hey, first year asshole."

The thudding sound my bottom created on the solid concrete pavement resulted in a few raised eyebrows from passersby. I ran and jumped on the first bus that came by.

"Hello, Mr. Engineer," greeted Anju when I finally reached her home. "Don't they teach you how to dress properly?" she asked, noticing my shabby appearance.

I told her about the plight of first-year students in a professional college and added a lot more to make a real sob story. The more I told her, the more she laughed, making me feel like an idiot. I did add that I had bunked just to be able to see her, and if my parents came to know about it, there would be more to pay than just a shabby appearance. She laughed even harder.

"Yeah, yeah," I retorted. "You girls don't have to bother about building a career. First you fleece your fathers, then your husbands. I wonder why God bothered to create females."

"So you boys could take care of us."

What could I say to that?

In May 1977, I appeared for the Marine Engineering entrance exam a few days later. Anju told me she had been praying for me. Confidentially, I went to a nearby temple and offered God a small bribe if He would help me succeed. To add a little weight to my request, I did add that I wanted it for Anju as well.

Three months later, I received a call for an interview.

"Wear a suit when you go for the interview," Anju cautioned me. "Anil says that it fetches more points."

"I don't have a suit."

"Well, at least wear a tie. I don't want to spend my life with a poorly-dressed mechanical engineer."

I was alone at home for the day. My parents had gone out visiting some relatives. Anju was on her *Dussehra* break and had come over to see me.

"Come, I'll show you something," I said as she sipped on a glass of Roohafza. I showed her a yellow envelope marked O.I.G.S. "Open it."

She did, and read the following:

Dear Sir,

We take great pleasure in informing you that you have been selected for the four-year Marine Engineering Training commencing on October 22nd, 1977. Kindly ...

"So, you're going?" she asked, as if she hadn't understood all along.

"Have to," I said. "My girlfriend wants me to be a marine engineer. What's the matter? Aren't you happy about it?"

She did not speak. I held her hand, squeezing it hard, then took her in my arms and pressed her close to me, hoping a little soothing would help. I don't know what happened, but she suddenly took my face in her hands and softly pressed her lips against mine – her warm, sweet, passionate lips in unison with mine. We stayed like that for a long time, content and lost in each other, for none of us knew how to proceed from there.

Epilogue
June 1983. London, England.

26

It is six months since Anju died, six months since a part of me died, too. Her remains were never found. I had been too much in shock to call her parents right away. Then, my ship sailed out ahead of schedule, and I never got a chance to visit them. I had called them from the next port, but none had known what to say. Now I have signed off my ship at Southampton and am visiting her parents. Together we reminisced over memories of the sweetest person who ever lived.

She is no more, but I remember everything about her vividly and always will.

I remember how she cried the day before my departure for Calcutta, how she kissed me and how I cried in bed that night before departing.

I was in Calcutta four years, coming home once a year for a month. On my first visit home, after completing nine months of training, I showed Anju photographs of myself in the Merchant Navy uniform. She seemed real proud of me.

During the second year of training, she wrote that her parents and mine had been getting together occasionally, and were planning to do something together during my next vacation. Sometime later she wrote that her father was planning to migrate to London, and he was quite excited about it. Her mother thought it would be great for Anju and her further education. I had a good mind to use my newly-acquired vocabulary and say "Balls", but I refrained. Instead, I simply wrote that if it made Anju happy, it also made me happy. She wrote back one word: "Balls!"

During my third year of training, she graduated from school, and stood first in the girls' section in all India. Also, that year when I came home during my vacation, the elders of both our families got together and ...

"Well, I guess that seals your fate," I said, as I slipped a ring over the third finger of her left hand.

Amidst clapping from our relatives, she whispered, "It seals your fate, too, Mister. Now, take your eyes off that cousin of mine."

Micky also came over for the occasion, from Poona, where he was undergoing training at the National Defence Academy.

Two days later, Anju left for London.

It was history. Everything was over for me. Somewhere in the distance, a clock sounded eleven gongs as I stood in my room at home. I had returned home to nothingness. At times I am tempted to question God. Why did our love story have to end like this? Why were two lovers never allowed to unite on earth? Would He answer, or was He made of stone –

immune to the feelings and pain of others? It seemed cruel.

I opened the drawer of my study table, and taking out a red folder, opened it carefully. They were all there, safe and well-preserved – Anju's letters.

"Dear Vicky," began one. "My dearest Vicky," said another. "Yours and yours only," ended another.

Somewhere, someone was singing, "Visions are there, In shades of blue, Smoking, shifting, leisurely drifting, My darling, I miss you so ..."

She is still there, and always will be, alive in my heart, alive to me. I ask myself, what it would be like if she had not died. And then I return to my dreams.

Only the visions are alive – visions of the past.

"I'll wait for you, Vicky, until I can join you," she wrote once.

I cry ... and wipe the tears that roll down my cheeks.

Life is not meant to be a brief candle, but a flaming torch. But sometimes, the flame dies ...

FACETS by PRADEEP GULATI

Published by Notion Press

A young escort in Phuket who has closed her heart to love...A wife, who is forced into prostitution by her husband, endeavours to escape as a stowaway on a ship...A man whose self-destructive infatuation towards a Bollywood star ruins many lives...An unorthodox love between an Indian and a coloured girl from the apartheid-ridden South Africa...A speech therapist who makes a differently-abled boy's dream a reality...A young boy who tries to understand the social stigma attached to rape...A seafarer in England who is saved from disaster on a treacherous night by a mysterious woman…An unassuming man who ends his life, but does not forget his wedding vows even at the moment of death…

How will you react to these characters?

Facets is an intriguing collection of fourteen irresistible short stories that look at various aspects of human relationships. Cleverly drawn from everyday characters and incidents from various parts of the world, these ingeniously plotted storylines have unexpected emotions and twists.